The author Chris Dann a Paramedic with over ....ce in the Ambulance service and co-author Tony Mock, ...ency Care Assistant with five years front line experience created the main character McDamnock TC.

 Initial intention was to come up with a nickname as a crew derived from their surnames Dann/ Mock, but words like 'Mock n Dann' didn't seem right. So from an anagram of their surnames, the word McDamnock eventually came about.

Making no sense as a tag name, but sounding more like a surname, an over the top Paramedic character was created instead. As it had a Scottish sound to it; then it was decided he came from the highlands. Then adding the authors Christian names; McDamnock TC was born, (no pun intended towards any Scottish people, in-fact both authors have a love for Scotland & its people). And yes for those that do the working out, there isn't enough M's or C's in their surnames and there's one too many n's, but it was at the end of a long nightshift when it popped into their heads). Anyway, a character had been created and eventually put into a story with staff's own real experiences.

With the exception of McDamnock and Billy; all other characters in this story are based around real people. No real names have been used and locations are fictional. Any resemblance to any person's name living or deceased is entirely coincidental.

 All the incidents attended in this story are based on real 999 emergencies that Paramedics have attended.

1

Chapter 1.

Chapter 2

Chapter 3

Chapter 4

Chapter 1.

McDamnock TC's

True blue light tales.

'Ye first McDamnock special brew Willie'

Billy, Billy Boyle that's me, or William Boyle as my father named me. Loved my parents, always hated the name though, I mean can you imagine the stick at school. But I survived and went onto college, drifting through my first few years of Science and Meds School before going onto Uni as my father wanted; concentrating on medicine. If he'd had his way I'd probably be nearly qualified as a Doctor by now, but it wasn't for me, all that studying; way too serious. Instead, I wasted a year or two before I finally got back on track and ended up doing a Paramedic science foundation degree.

Studying to become a Paramedic was a little different, a bit more of a hands on approach, but still so many lectures to sit through and a hell of a lot seemed too in-depth and pointless to learn, I mean it's not as though we're gonna be Doctors. However, some of the other students made it all the more interesting by their antics. *'What goes on the course, stays on the course'* as several of them kept saying. I myself was a good boy of course. Didn't get drunk, well not too drunk. Didn't misbehave and wasn't in bed too late, well no later than two in the morning and definitely on my own. I do have a girlfriend back home who I love, but it was obvious some of the others didn't with the way they were carrying on. It was amazing to see how they got through their exams; with their self-inflicted sleep deprivation and hangovers.

Anyway, I've made it to twenty four years of age now and have passed my Paramedic science degree with honours. My Dad bless him said he was happy for me and looked it at my passing out ceremony, but still managed to say through gritted teeth: *'you done well son, but could have done better as a*

Doctor.' Nice...Is all I can think of to sum-up my father's quote on my proudest day.

Well you would have thought that's it I'm a Paramedic now, but no, not yet. You have to apply to a trust and still have to complete a year on the front line before becoming fully qualified. So after applying to several trusts, I've been accepted by the North West Ambulance Service and am on my way to work in Cumbria. There's still a lot to learn that training school didn't teach. But as for today, today is my first day out on the road. I've been told I'm one of the lucky ones, as I've been given a three month secondment. Everyone else is pissed off that they're going all over the place as reliefs, working at various stations.

My tutor told me *'It's good to have the chance to get your feet under the table and work with just one Paramedic, before being sent out there and everywhere with different staff. Like a lamb set amongst wolves'* he said, smiling at his own peculiar sense of humour. So I'm going to a quaint little sleepy village I've never heard of called Casildon-on-the-Hill and I'm to work with an experienced Paramedic, though I did hear someone say *'more like it'll be an experience working with this one.'*

It's early! Bloody early, as I manage to find this ambulance station that's hidden out of sight, tucked away down a tiny lane off the high road. Though I'm not starting till six in the morning, I pull into the car park at five twenty for my first twelve hour shift. I get out looking all keen, but with an obvious shyness surrounding me as I walk up to the station entrance wearing my brand new unspoilt non faded uniform. It's quiet with only one response car parked outside. The station looks a little bit tired to say the least and in need of some modernisation, but it has a cosy feel about it.

As I walk in I'm greeted by a Paramedic looking a bit weary; he's at the end of a long and busy nightshift on the rapid response car. 'Hi, you must be the newbie, I'm Phil.'

'Billy' I reply shaking his hand.

'Well Billy fancy a tea? The night crew's still out at the moment, not been back all night.' He tells me walking off to the kitchen.

'Yes please' I reply as I sit down and wait nervously, looking around at the station messroom, thinking of what to say while he's out there.

He walks in with two teas. 'Here you go,' passing me an old looking mug before he sits down keeping one eye on the worn out wall clock. It's obvious he's ready to get to his bed after another demanding night.

Inquisitive to know about my mentor I ask: 'So what's my crewmate like?' He gulps on his tea, smiles and says 'hmm...you'll see.' We sit and he chats about how a shift generally goes, although he seems reluctant to return to the question about my new crewmate, which leaves me even more curious as to what this Para I'm to work with will be like.

Then a loud thunderous and rumbling engine noise is heard, as an old classic dark green Jag roars into the car park at speed and comes to a sudden halt. With a loud bang from the rear followed by a cloud of exhaust smoke, a tall figure gets out waving his hand through the smoke as he makes his way over.

He walks in and stands in the doorway to the messroom with his hands on his hips. He's tall, at least six foot tall and well-built with broad shoulders. He looks to be in his fifties as he stands there sporting a brown wavy hair style that has a tinge of ginger running through it. But my eyes are immediately drawn to his big bushy eyebrows that seem to have a life of their own as they rise up before he speaks. 'Well hello there laddie...You must be me new wee crewmate' he says in a strong Scottish voice, before walking over to me and extending his arm out to greet me. I get up and raise my hand in return. He grasps it and shakes my hand vigorously. His big hairy hand nearly shaking my hand off the arm it's attached to. So strong is his grip I'm almost pulled forward as I feel the force of his welcoming handshake vibrating through my body.

'McDamnock TC's me name' he thunderously states.

'Billy's mine' I nervously reply.

'Aye it's good to meet ya Willie, we'll look after you,' he says.

'No, my names Billy.'

'Aye Willie I heard ya...Now I need a strong mug of McDamnock brew' he says as he walks off towards the kitchen. As I sit back down scary images of the next three months run through my mind. I look at Phil who smiles at me and as if he's been reading my mind says 'you'll be fine.'

In the kitchen the sound of cups and spoons clanging, can be heard, followed by the loudest and longest stirring of tea ever. The stirring gets faster and faster as if done by an old cranky machine. Then with a final clanging of the spoon against the sink as if McDamnock's playing drums out there; he finishes off with the sound of a 'musical drum fill at the end of a bar,' before finally walking into the messroom. The two mugs of tea swirling all over the place, but somehow managing to stay un-spilt, as McDamnock heads straight for me.

'Here you go laddie try a McDamnock special brew. Bet you haven't tried anything as good as this before,' he says as he shoves it in-front of me. I politely, but reluctantly take the tea even though I've just finished one. I look down into the large mug, the dark coloured liquid resembling a very, very strong coffee with a smell rising up that seems as if it'll numb your taste buds upon receiving. I think to myself *'you're right I haven't tried anything like it.'*

Fortunately I had noticed it was now past our start time, so before attempting to taste it I ask the question 'does the vehicle always get back late?' As I try to take my mind off of the mug of liquid in front of me that would even shame a builder's mug of tea.

'You'll never get home to your lassie on time doing this job son' he replies. 'This ain't like that Holby or Casualty shite on the TV...This is the real world of the emergency service you're in now. Just when you think you know what you're going to it'll come up and bite ya on the bahooky. But don't you fret laddie, old Mac's by your side.' Then reclining in his lazy-boy armchair he starts to read his newspaper while holding his large mug of McDamnock brew with one hand on his chest. Occasionally he lets go licking his fingers to turn the pages as the mug is left to balance between his chin and chest. He slurps loudly at his mug of tea, leaving me to sit there and wonder what I've let myself in for.

Forty five minutes pass, before the night crew finally return. There's a quick hand-over of keys, radios and a piece of paper with a list of equipment needed to replenish the Ambulance, before they quickly walk on out. 'Hi nice to meet you, sorry in a hurry' one of them says as she rushes out the door; I've not even had time to introduce myself before they've gone.

Then the radio goes off, our first job of the day. Shaking his head as he walks out to the vehicle McDamnock says aloud 'those twallys can't wait to get us out there, without even knowing if we've got everything we need.

I quickly follow on behind, trying to keep up with his big strides. 'What's a twally?' I ask, unable to recall anyone mentioning a twally in training school.

'It's me pet name Willie for those at the other end of the radio. Twallys, you know the dispatchers.'

'Oh I see' I reply thinking; this is going to be a complicated day.

In the Ambulance, McDamnock's rummaging through the grab-bag. 'I'll be good to you me laddie, not fair to make you jump in at the deep end and put your skills to the test yet. I'll do the attending, let you see how it's done and ease you into the job...But then after the first one it's all yours Willie, but don't worry your wee head off, I won't let you make a twally of yourself' he says jokingly, laughing at his own sense of humour as he pats me on the back.

'Sure...Whatever you thinks best' I answer back with a smile, pretending to find his joke humorous and think now would be a good moment to go and check the vehicle. So with keys in hand I get out of the back and go round to the cab. Sitting in the driver's seat I adjust it till I'm comfy, start the engine and turn on the blue-lights. Walking round the vehicle checking they all work, I'm reminded of what our driving instructor told us; *'don't worry you'll always have time to do a full vehicle check first thing.' 'Yer right that's a load of bollocks really looks as if that ever happens...Not.'* At the back I notice the fleet number 0642 *making a mental note of it as I complete my* lap round.

With all the lights flashing how they should, I get back in and sit there nervously waiting as McDamnock gets in the other side.

'Ok laddie, nice and smooth' he tells me. 'No need to drive like a goon.'

'Sure nice and smooth' I reply; thinking *'this'll be ok he can't be that bad, surely he won't bite my head off about my driving'* as I put it in drive and we head out of the station, my first drive with blue lights on.

Feeling really nervous, I try to concentrate on making our way to the job, but my mind's taken off that by McDamnock's booming words of advice resonating through my left ear on; 'the ways of the road' as he calls it.

'The thing you need to learn me lad about the wee drivers of Casildon is that they'll go one of three ways, either they'll go our way, their way, or any bloody way, but they'll still be in our way…A quick blast of the tartan trumpet will clear 'em out of the way.'

I had no idea what a 'tartan trumpet' meant and couldn't even get a word in edgeways to ask, so could only hope; it was his reference to the two tones.

His constructive criticism continued all the way, the only interruptions, came from updates on the job we were going to. 'It's an elderly lass down' McDamnock chirpily yells, 'It says she's on the floor with query a fractured hip.' Then that sentence was quickly followed by 'go left laddie. Now right. Now in-between them. Go round the outside of them. Give em a blast on the tartan trumpet, speed up…No slow down laddie, the wee lass isn't going anywhere.'

As we arrive in the street of the patient's address, I look for a parking space and the only one I see big enough for our ambulance, is further down the road. As I make my way past the patient's address towards the space, McDamnock yells out;

'Willie where you going, no time for parking up the bloody road it's an emergency, park outside the house, in the middle of the bloody street!'

I stop the ambulance as McDamnock requested, in 'the middle of the bloody road outside the patient's address.' He quickly jumps out shouting 'aye good going me lad, good going.'

Feeling lightheaded with a ringing sound still going through my ears after that driving tutorial, I sit there for a moment thinking back to being told 'and I'm the lucky one to get a secondment.'

Chapter 1

The wee lassie down incident.

'Sabulba and nuggets with that Willie?'

Billy gets out of the cab, *'God my head's pounding and I ain't even seen a patient yet'* he thinks to himself as he walks up to the front door where McDamnock is kneeling, peering through the letter box. He's calling to the patient, as there's been no answer when he pressed the bell. 'Can you hear me lassie? It's the ambulance' he shouts. A quiet voice replies 'help I'm on the floor, help' continually repeated over and over.

'Aye lassie we'll have you up in a jiffy,' McDamnock replies through the letter box. 'Wot did I tell you Willie, The lass has fallen behind locked doors and those twally dispatchers, can't be bothered to tell us the key safe code before we get here. You have a chat through the letter box me boy; keep the lassie calm while I'll call them up for the code.'

Billy opens the letter box to try his first attempt at speaking to a patient, even though it's one he cannot even see, but as he looks through to see if he can spot her, a set of gnarling teeth suddenly appear at the other side of the box jumping up and snapping. Startled, Billy falls backwards onto the grass.

'Willie, no time to be acting dafty like a jessy sitting down on your bahooky' McDamnock shouts as he passes him by; on his way to the front door again.

'Think I'll wait till the door's open' Billy insists, still startled by that close encounter with those teeth.

With the key safe code obtained, the box is soon opened and with key in hand McDamnock opens the front door. Billy stands cautiously further back waiting for the thing the teeth belonged to, to head straight for McDamnock. As the door opens a little Jack Russell comes running out, jumping up and wagging its tail looking happy to see him. *'Typical'* Billy whispers to himself, thinking *'it looked much bigger than that through the letter box.'*

 As they enter the house another dog appears from nowhere; nearly tripping Billy over. The weight of the fully loaded grab bag hanging over Billy's shoulder; causes him to lose his balance as he tries to avoid its collision course. An old looking pug dog, beige with black spots on circles them before trotting off, making a constant snorting sound as it sniffs the ground. Looking more like a pig truffle hunting, it makes its way from one room to the next sounding like a chugging combustion engine, it doesn't even pause to take a breath as it constantly snorts every square inch of the floor.

McDamnock and Billy look at each other bemused by the strange behaviour of the creature and amazed how this thing doesn't keel over from oxygen starvation. Then, back to finding their patient McDamnock calls out into the house;

'Peak a boo lassie where are you.'

'Help me, I'm on the floor' cries the patient from the bathroom.

'Aye lassie we're on our way,' McDamnock replies to the voice as they head in the direction from which it came. In the bathroom, they find an elderly lady sat on the floor resting against the toilet.

'Oh help me please, help me it hurts' the now tired and distressed voice cries out and immediately begins crying upon seeing the two ambulance men in her bathroom doorway.

'Hey lass we're here now,' McDamnock softly tells the patient in a tone Billy hadn't heard from him before. McDamnock's normally gruff and loud voice; replaced by a calming gentle tone.

'What's your name?' he asks.

'Annie' she quietly replies.

'So Annie, why are you crying?'

She sobs 'I didn't think anyone heard me when I fell, I pressed my care-line button, but I couldn't hear anybody and thought no one was coming. I've never had to use it before and I've messed myself as well' she says tearfully.

'No don't you worry we'll help sort that out and as far as your care-line button goes, if they can't hear you they'll still send us lot out to you, just in case something's happened and just as-well they did hey Annie,' McDamnock says to her trying to give her some reassurance. 'Now Annie did you trip or did you feel unwell before you fell' he asks trying to find out the cause of her fall.

'I was on my way to the toilet' she tells him. 'When I think I lost my balance...I think it was Sabulba that got in the way, he's always getting under my feet,' she explains still weeping. 'Aye he looks a wee handful of a dog doesn't he,' thinking to himself '*the pesky thing's gone utterly mad.*'

'Ok Annie we'll get you off the floor soon, but we need to do a few checks first.

On assessing Annie's legs, she begins to complain of pain in her left hip and is unable to bend her knee. 'It hurts and I can't lift it' Annie tells him.

He's already noticed the position of her left leg when they walked in, but looks back down at the shortened leg displaced outwards and rotated at the foot. 'Sorry Annie, but I think you might have a fracture to your hip so it's gonna have to be a trip up to A&E for you I'm afraid' he gentle tells her.

At that point the pug dog comes back into the bathroom, snorting and sniffing away at the floor as it makes its way from corner to corner.

'Sabulba' Annie cries. 'Get out will you.' Billy lifts it up and escorts it out and into the living-room, but struggles to get the living-room door shut before Sabulba comes snorting back out in a hurry.

While he's wrestling with the pug and the door McDamnock calls out. 'Willie while you're out there can you get me the Entonox please...And think we'll need some Morphine too' he shouts out.

'Yep will do once I've got this thing out of the way' Billy replies. *'If it'll keep still long enough for me to close the door'* he whispers to himself.

'Aye, thanks laddie.'

Not winning the battle with Sabulba, Billy picks it up and holds it at arm's length as it tries to wriggle and snort him. Escorting him to the far end of the living-room, he quickly makes his way out before the pug can snort its way back to the door. *'There, that's one dog dealt with at least we won't have him snorting around us anymore'* Billy thinks to himself.

Returning back to the bathroom with Entonox and Morphine, Billy sees McDamnock inserting a cannula into a small vein in the back of Annie's hand. He looks on impressed with McDamnock's smooth action, as the cannula is swiftly inserted with hardly any discomfort to Annie. His fingertips smoothly glide the needle back as the canula is advanced fully into the vein.

With Morphine drawn up McDamnock gives a small amount to start with. 'There you go lassie, a wee drop of this stuff will make you forget about that aching hip.'

Giving the Morphine a few minutes to take effect, they clean Annie as best they can without further injuring her. Then McDamnock passes Billy three triangular dressing slings.

'Surely we're not gonna put her arms into slings as-well are we? Billy asks looking at him confused.

'All that medical stuffs they teach you nowadays in that university' he answers Billy, shaking his head. 'Nae laddie, let me show you...You get one sheet between the knees; we don't want Annie's legs knocking together now do we. Then tie a dressing around the hips Willie to support them, another around the knees laddie, give a little support there too and finally a third one around the ankles. Bet they didn't teach you that in training school, that's old school stuff Willie.'

Once Annie's all wrapped up, they lift her onto the carry chair.

'Annie what medication do you take,' McDamnock asks.

'Oh I don't know, I can't remember at the moment' she answers back worried why she's unable to think.

'Don't worry lassie, you've had an eventful morning so far and maybe the morphine's not helping. Do you know where your prescription list then? We could do with taking that with us' McDamnock asks.

'Oh that's in the kitchen she happily tells him, looking a little high as the Morphine's obviously doing its job. With McDamnock at the back of the carry chair and Billy holding Annie's legs out straight, so as not to cause more damage or pain to her hip injury, they head to the kitchen with Annie humming to herself as they go.

In the kitchen, Billy's unable to find anything to rest her legs on to keep them level, so he ends up bending over and holding her legs from underneath, while feeling around on the work surfaces for a prescription list. The Jack Russell now hearing them rustle about, runs into the kitchen and heads straight for Billy's behind inquisitively smelling his rear. Feeling the wet snout prodding him from behind Billy starts to worry about those teeth again while he's trying to look for the list. 'They really didn't teach us anything like this at Uni' Billy whispers to his crewmate.

'Aye laddie the tutors of today' McDamnock quietly replies. 'They only focus on the dramatic stuffs and not how to deal with holding up a pair of elderly lady's legs such as Annie, while being prodded by a Jack Russell as you look for a prescription. Lassie are you sure it's in here' McDamnock asks her, now Billy's searched everywhere.

'Oh mmm... maybe it's on the table in the living-room then' she chuckles as she continues to hum her tune. A frustrated Billy looks up at McDamnock whose eyebrows show his own frustration. So turning around they wheel Annie out of the kitchen quickly followed by the Jack Russell as they head for the living-room.

No sooner are they in there when Sabulba the pug who's been oblivious to the fact he's been shut in all alone, heads straight for them. Still looking like he's truffle hunting, he snorts at the ground as he circles around them, while the Jack Russell leaps onto the furniture and jumps back and forth amongst the sofa and armchairs. Laughing at the two men surrounded by her dogs, Annie begins to think that maybe it's not on the table.

'I think maybe it's fallen down the side of the sofa.'

They head for an armchair and Billy rests Annie's legs on the cushion, giving himself a quick breather.

'Oh young man, are you trying to sweep me off my feet' she giggles to him.

Billy now feeling exhausted from all the bending over looks up at Annie. 'Annie I'm gonna need to rest your legs a while so I can have another look for your prescription. Otherwise I'm gonna need to sit down.'

'Oh that's a shame, just when I was getting used to this. It's been a long time since I had a young man at my feet.'

'Lassie we'll just have a wee pause then we'll carry on dancing, this lad's got more stamina than both of us,' McDamnock tells her as he puts his hand on her shoulder reassuring her that they'll get back to wheeling her around shortly.

Going over to the sofa Billy puts his hand down the small gap between the sofa and armchair. Unable to see anything and having to rely on feel his face suddenly changes from curiosity to one of worry as he slowly lifts his hand back up. Worried about what it is he's put his hand into his face now goes from worry to shock, as he's hand reveals a dark brown mess stuck to his glove. He looks over at the Jack Russell who looks back at him, tilting his head for a moment before carrying on furniture hoping. Not inquisitive enough to know what's attached to his glove, he decides to just hold his hand out away from him.

'Ah that's where my maltesers went' Annie says and chuckles with laughter. With a sigh of relief Billy takes the malteser covered glove off and then pulls the sofa out, not wanting to take any more chances. Now with a better view he can see what's down there. He sorts through the collection of magazines, picking up more maltesers and placing them in front of the sofa so they don't get squashed. Just then Sabulba sniffs his way over. Smelling the maltesers and pushes them to one side he tries to get his nose down where Billy's hand is and begins to push his head against the sofa. Snorting and sniffing at the gap he's making Billy's attempt to find the prescription harder.

'Willie what you doing, truffle hunting with the dog? Come on, no time for mucking about.'

'I think I've got it' Billy says, as he lifts the prescription list up. Regaining his composure after the struggle with the sofa and Sabulba, Billy returns to holding Annie's legs. 'Right, we ready then.'

McDamnock presses Annie's care-line button to inform them that they're taking her to A&E and asking them to let Annie's daughter know. 'Oh and also, she needs to come and sort out the pesky dogs too' he adds. 'Think we'll leave your pendant up out the way of the dogs Annie, otherwise if they get their snouts on it they'll be pressing it all night long.'

They quickly make their way out of the living-room, shutting the door behind before the dogs escape.

'You're not going to leave my dogs trapped in there are you' Annie asks concerned.

'We'll let them out once we've got you out Annie' McDamnock says assuring her that they haven't forgotten about them. 'But first where's your door key?'

Annie just stares at Billy for a moment, smiling at him as he's bent forward holding her legs level.

'Oh you are a handsome young man, if I were only a few years younger I'd be chasing after you.'

'When you get out of Hospital Annie, you can chase after him all you like' McDamnock says. 'Now what about that door key lassie?'

'Oh yes' she finally answers now her mind's back with the current situation, even though her face still looks as though she's dreaming of Billy. 'Hmmm...I think it's in my coat by the front door.'

Billy puts his hand inside the pocket, hoping not to find any more maltesers. 'Yep I've got it' thinking to himself *'thank-god that was easier than looking for the prescription list.'*

As they head out to the ambulance several neighbours are curtain twitching, looking out of their windows wanting to know who's going into the ambulance that's blocking their road.

'They'll all be gossiping about me you know, maybe I should have brought my sunglasses' Annie says.

'Don't worry lassie, just give them a wave.'

Freeing one hand from under the blanket Annie smiles as she gives them a royal wave while they make their way to the tail-lift. Once inside they gently lift her onto the trolley. Billy gets out and watches all the curtain twitchers begin to step away from their windows now that the excitement's over while he stows the tail-lift away.

'Ouch it's starting to hurt again' Annie says as the Morphine's starting to wear off.

'Aye lassie, we'll check your BP first and give ya a wee drop more then,' McDamnock says to Annie then looks over at Billy standing beside the back door. 'Here ye go Willie don't forget to put these back into the key safe after you've let the dogs out and locked the door' as he chucks Billy the keys.

'Thanks, so I get to deal with the dogs again.'

'Annie needs a drop more Morphine laddie and besides you've built up a good relationship with em, I don't wanna spoil that' he replies with a smile.

Billy opens the living-room door slowly and leaves it ajar as he quickly makes his way towards the front door. The Jack Russell's the first to nudge it open enough to get out into the hallway, followed by the pug snorting the floor as he follows. It's close, but Billy manages to make it to the front door and shut it behind before the two dogs reach him. With a sigh of relief he locks it before replacing the spare key in the key safe. The two dogs left to continue guarding the letter box and carry on truffle hunting alone. Getting back to their vehicle Billy opens the back door to check everything's ok.

'Aye laddie Annie's away with the fairies again; missing you already she is, wanting to know where you'd got to, but we're ready now...a nice and smooth drive Willie that's what we want, nice and smooth.'

Billy tries to make the ride as smooth as possible, knowing every little bump will be felt in the back, especially by someone with a fractured bone. *'Remember: accelerator sense...Accelerator sense!'* his driving instructor kept shouting on their driving course, verbally ramming the idea down their throats as the students were thrown from side to side in the back of the Ambulance as it drove around the bends.

'Ouch,' McDamnock shouts as he suddenly sits back down on his seat, just when he was trying to get up. Billy had forgotten about the back wheels while driving over a speed bump.

'Sorry about that' He embarrassingly replies.

'Think it's my turn to stay sat on me bahooky' McDamnock jokingly tells him.

Parking in the ambulance bay at Casildon General Hospital, Billy thinks to himself *'well that could have gone smoother.'* 'Think I need to work on that a bit more' he tells McDamnock as he opens the back door.

'No worries laddie we're still in one piece' he replies as he looks at a happy Annie, who's just been given some more Morphine and is smiling at Billy.

'Ah there's my young man, I was beginning to think you wasn't coming back' a contented Annie tells him.

As they take her inside Billy gets his first sight of a busy A& E department with doctors and nurses hurrying around. He pays particular attention to McDamnock's hand-over to the nurse in charge; as he gives her his handover:

• This lovely lady's Annie, 78 years old.

• Tripped over pet while going to toilet.

•No loss of consciousness.

• Complaining of left hip pain, with shortness and rotation to leg. Looks like left neck of femur fracture.

• 10mg morphine given.

'Ok cubicle fourteen please,' she says to them.

Entering the cubicle McDamnock asks 'Did they show you how to use a pat slide Willie?'

'No we heard about it, but wasn't able to practice with one.'

'No worries laddie, old Mac will give you a quick master-class.' He tells Billy where the white plastic slide board is kept, providing someone hasn't left it laying about, which then causes the nurses to run around like headless chickens, panicking when it's needed in resus. 'Right Annie, cross your arms we'll do it all for you' he tells her while Billy lays the board onto the hospital trolley. 'Ok Willie I'll roll Annie onto her side, you put the board underneath and then we'll slide across to you. But Willie, don't forget to take Annie's legs with you, got that laddie? To me...To you.'

Nodding in reply, Billy thinks *'I've no idea if I'm meant to take him serious or not.'*

Following McDamnock's instructions they transfer Annie across and make her comfortable again.

'You take care now lassie all the best,' McDamnock says as he goes off to book her in at reception.

'Oh do you have to go too,' she asks Billy with a sad face.

'Afraid so Annie, but the nurse will be here in a moment.'

She grabs hold of Billy's shirt collar, pulls him down to her level and gives him a smacker of a kiss on his cheek.

'Now you behave yourself young man' she says.

'I will do Annie,' Billy replies with red cheeks as he straightens up his shirt.

Just then a young male nurse opens the curtain and enters the cubicle, Annie's face lights up again as she looks at him.

'I think you'll be ok now Annie' Billy says, having noticed her next conquest.

'I think so too' she replies to Billy with a wink.

Smiling at Annie, Billy walks off with their trolley back to 0642 to wipe it down, tidy up and reflect on his first job with McDamnock TC.

Chapter 1.

The reality is more sombre than the tale contained within.

Ok laddie you ready?

'I guess so' Billy replies now sat in the attendant's seat.

'Let's see what the twallys have for us then and call me Mac, nae not McDamnock; sounds too serious.'

Billy Presses the clear button on the terrafix touch screen, *'the all singing and dancing satellite navigation computer system and relaying information thingy'* as Mac calls it. *'It'll do everything, too good for me liking Willie. What is wrong with a map book and a conversation over the radio I ask you?'* Then Billy puts his first cell call in on his handset to dispatch and sits back in the chair feeling slightly nervously as he waits for the reply, while going over in his mind what he's got to say. *'EA0642 green at Casildon General...EA0642 green at Casildon General.'*

The radio goes off and Billy holds it up to his mouth. 'EA 6042 yellow...I mean green.'

'No time to be going through the colours of the rainbow laddie' Mac quickly interrupts.

'Errm...Errm...' Billy continues to say into the radio, as Mac's reply has amused him and made him lose his train of thought.

'Here laddie let me help ya; we don't want you looking like a twally to the twallys' he says trying to help out. 'Naught sex four two, green Casildon' booms Mac's voice on his handset.

'Roger 0642, details of a Red call coming through, backing up a car.'

Billy presses the mobile button on the terrafix. 'Looks like we're going to a Sixty six year old female, difficulty in breathing, at Silver Hares nursing home.'

'Oh aye that's one of our regulars; Casildon's largest nursing home that one is' Mac says as he speeds off out of the hospital and on towards the hills of Casildon. Weaving through the traffic Mac continues with some more informative driving tips. 'Willie you see, the dafty folk of Casildon will slow down for us, but won't stop. They expect us to overtake on two wheels if needed, as if we're Starsky and Hutch.'

'Who?' Billy replies.

'Oh aye wee bit before your time…The point is laddie they think we'll go flying round them like on TV, all dramatic and stuff.'

'Right,' Billy answers back while trying to sit still as Mac's enthusiastic driving causes him to reach up with his left hand to the handle above the door and hold on. His right hand then begins to grip the armrest as he slides from one side of the seat to the other while Mac steers sharply round the bends. Then his heavy breaking jolts Billy forward against the seat belt before he's thrown back against the seat as Mac accelerates off again.

'You see laddie the lassie coming towards us has stopped, but the one in front of us…Nae she won't. She'll keep on going unaware of what's behind in her rear view mirror. You mark my words laddie, when she does see us; she'll just slow down and then we won't be able to squeeze through the gap with the car that's stopped on the other side.'

Billy nods, trying hard to concentrate on Mac's second driving tutorial as they press on.

'Where you from Willie, I can tell it's not from around these parts' Mac asks, while sat in his casual driving position giving the tartan trumpet a blast.

'Wraysbury in Berkshire originally' Billy explains. 'Samantha my fiancée and I grew up there, before we went to Uni.'

'So how come you've ended up in this wee village then?' Mac asks inquisitively as he shakes his head at a car that's just pulled out in front of him.

'Well she studied law and was offered a job nearby, so here we are.'

'Aye young love, ain't it grand Willie?' Mac says glancing at his crewmate with a smile. 'Well the thing you gotta understand about the folk of Casildon-On-The-Hill, is they either think they're too sick to call for the Doctor, or well...They actually are too sick...Too sick to even pray laddie' Mac says while swerving his way through the traffic.

 Turning into Silver Hares nursing home Mac pulls up sharply next to the response car, leaps out and makes his way up to the front door. Whereas Billy, with head still spinning gets out whispering to himself: *'Christ this is gonna be a long three months.'*

'Don't forget to press at scene on the terrafix' Mac calls out, just as Billy's shut the door. Turning around again he opens it and leans in reaching for the display screen *'A very long three months.'*

Meeting Mac at the double glass reception doors, he's already peering through as there's no answer yet. 'Everytime Willie, they take ages to answer everytime.'

Eventually a member of staff arrives in reception, rushing to open the door she apologises for the delay as she lets them in.

'Nae don't worry lass, I know you're a wee bit busy...Where we going then.'

'Oh I don't know, I'll ask the manager. RITA' she shouts out in the direction of the office.

'WHAT' comes the reply.

'There's two young men for you.'

'I'm busy, tell them to come back this afternoon.'

'They're ambulance men Rita. 'I'm sorry about this' she tells them. 'She's always busy.'

'Hmm...Sounds like it' Mac replies.

'Oh hello gents' Rita says apologetic as she comes over. Let me take you to your colleague.' Leading the way, she gives them some bad news. 'I'm sorry boys, but she's passed away.'

'That was sudden then' Mac says sounding surprised. 'I thought she was having breathing problems when we were called. I'm sorry to hear that lass.'

'Sheila had only been with us a few days...You see she hand dementia and was in here for respite while her husband was away visiting family.'

At that moment they enter the lounge to see their colleague kneeling down beside Sheila performing CPR.

'I don't think she's left us just yet' Mac says to Rita as he and Billy quickly make their way over to them. 'Willie, this is Sue' Mac says introducing them as Billy takes over chest compressions.

'Hi Sue.'

'Hello my lovely' she replies in a Norfolk accent. 'So, on my arrival they tell me she'd passed away, but when I saw Sheila she was still breathing, though very shallow, her sats were only 70% and her chest was very congested. But within a couple of minutes she went into respiratory arrest and there's been no pulse now for about a minute.'

Mac gets the intubation kit ready and gains IV access in Sheila's arm. 'You ok laddie? He asks his crewmate.

'Yes Mac, I'm ok' Billy answers back, even though he didn't have time to prepare himself for his first cardiac arrest. This is the first time Billy's ever seen a lifeless body, but he doesn't have time to take it all in, only that the chest compressions on a real person ain't anything like on resus Annie in training school.

'Let's swap over mee cocker' sue says to Billy as it's time for a rhythm check.

'Got an output I think Mac' Billy says as he looks at the wave form on the monitor and feels a weak but palpable carotid pulse.

'Aye laddie yer right there,' Mac replies looking at the monitor too.

Sue stops compressions and waits to see if the pulse falls again.

'I can still feel it above 60' Billy says as he counts a minute's worth. 'And I think she's making some respiratory effort too' noticing her chest start to rise between his ventilation with the bag and mask. Sheila begins to gag on the i-gel airway that's protecting her airway.

'Take it out laddie, let's see if she's maintaining her own airway.'

With chest compressions ceased and only the smaller OPA in place to help protect Sheila's airway, they pause for a moment to assess their patient's condition post cardiac arrest.

'Ok boys, shall we get a blood pressure and ECG done, and if that's ok get ready to load and go.'

'Aye Suzie.'

'I wish you'd stop calling me Suzie, you know it annoys me.'

'Aye, I know.'

'Oh you can be so irritating.'

'Suzie you're just too easy to wind up.'

'Children while you're bickering' Billy says. I'll go get the trolley shall I.' He leaves the two of them to continue their petty conversation as they obtain a BP and ECG and heads back to reception. But, the home is more like a maze as one corridor looks like another. *'For F... sake, I'm sure I've just been this way!'* Billy thinks to himself as he turns around again still looking for reception. *'Not only are all the carpets the same pattern as the wallpaper, but I'm sure all the picture frames have the same bloody pictures in.'* Seeing a carer up ahead walking out of a patient's room, Billy rushes up to her. 'Excuse me, but I'm a bit lost.'

'And where would such a fine young man like to go' the mature carer's voice replies.

'I'm heading for reception, I need to get our bed.'

'Mmm...I'll take you then' she says with a smile. Walking slowly along the corridor she keeps looking him up and down. 'Not seen you before, you're new aren't you.'

'My first day,' Billy replies a little concerned that their progress towards reception is a little too slow.

'Well I hope we get to see a lot more of you.'

'I'm sure you will' he retorts. 'But can we go a bit faster, my colleagues are in a hurry.'

'For you sugar, anything.'

As they quickly make progress to reception Billy thinks to himself: *'Work in the country they say, out in the sticks; it'll be quiet, nothing ever happens, it'll be hassle free. I'm not even half way through my first day and I've got a patient who's just come back from an arrest, two colleagues probably wondering where the hell I've got to and now I've got a cougar pouncing on me.'*

At the vehicle Billy lowers the trolley down on the tailift, he's aware that his new admirer is probably eyeing him up and down as she watches him closely from the reception door.

'Shall I give you a hand?' she asks as Billy struggles to push the trolley through the entrance door.

'If you don't mind' Billy replies trying not to say anything that will lead her on. The journey back to the his colleagues is a lot shorter than the one back to the ambulance and as she holds the lounge door open for Billy she winks.

'I'm just down the corridor if you need any more assistance, just shout Honey.'

'Huh? Billy replies.

'That's my name sweetie' she tells him pointing to her name badge before walking off.

'Oh got ya' Billy realises as he pushes the trolley through the doors and heads over to his colleagues in the lounge.

'I'm gonna take that razor out of the monitor's pouch in a minute and shave those damn eyebrows of yours off.'

'Nae lassie, no one touches these wee beasties,' is the sound that Billy hears upon his return with the trolley as Mac's still winding Sue up.

'Yous still at it?'

'No Billy my lovely' Sue tells him. 'Mac's just a little sensitive about his eyebrows...Anyway Sheila's BP and ECG are all ok, she's still maintaining a good respiratory effort and cardiac output so we should be ok to transfer.

'Come on Mac, put some effort into it will you' Sue tells him as she pulls the trolley along the corridor towards reception while Billy follows on with Sue's equipment.

'Suzie, if I push any faster you'll be run over, you need to put a wee bit more effort into pulling.'

Finally at the ambulance, Billy chucks Sue's equipment in the boot of her car and rushes over to help transfer up and into the back of the ambulance. Another BP to make sure Sheila's cardiac output is still sufficient and Mac gives the keys to Billy.

'Do you want an experienced pair of hands to come with ya Mac?' Sue asks before getting out.

'Why do you know anyone Suzie?'

'Oh you're so funny, I take that as you and those eyebrows of yours are capable of managing then...Well boys well done and Billy it's nice to meet you' Sue says getting out. Following on Billy gets out and shuts the back door 'Oh and Billy' Sue adds as he's about to go around to the cab. 'You'll deserve a medial if you make it through the next three months with this old git, drive safely, see you soon' she says getting in her car.

'Ok laddie nice and smooth this time, mind those bumps.'

'Will do Mac' Billy replies as they set off on blues to Casildon General.

But back in the real world.

They leave resus with a job well done, not many patients that go into cardiac arrest in the community make it to A&E with a cardiac output and even less make it there breathing on their own. But this is where the tale takes a sombre turn. Unknown to Mac and Billy; who return to Casildon General several more times that day, Sheila never regained consciousness. Sue, Mac and Billy done their best to keep her brain perfused with oxygenated blood, but sometimes that's just not enough. She was taken to a ward where she sadly passed away the next day.

But, sometimes life gives in small ways. Because Sue, Mac and Billy were able to bring her into resus still breathing. This allowed enough time for her husband and two sons to be informed of the bad news and travel back to Casildon where they spent the last few hours of Sheila's life beside her bed, her husband holding her hand as her two sons watched their mum slip away. It maybe a small mercy, but it's a big thing to a family, something that in-time helps with the loss.

Chapter 1

David's incident.

'You'll be fine with this one Willie.'

Sat in the attendant's seat again Billy calls up despatch. The next job comes through and gives Mac a smile as he reads out the details displayed on the terrafix: 'forty nine year old male with a PR bleed. A bleed from the bahooky Willie...This one's all yours, should be a good one for you to get stuck into' he says as he puts his foot to the floor and 0642 speeds off out of Casildon General.

Turning into the patient's road 0642 comes to a sudden halt in the middle of the road, right outside the address. At the front door with grab-bag in hand Billy rings the doorbell. A tall, slightly overweight gentleman opens it; looking very uncomfortable as he fidgets from side to side.

'Oh I'm so glad you're here lads I've never had anything like this before,' he says with a quivering voice.

'Go and have a sit down sir' Billy says to try and calm him down. The patient quickly turns round and like a shot is gone, headed for the lounge before they even enter the hall way.

Once they catch up they find him sat down in his armchair leaning to one side. Billy kneels down beside and asks 'What's your name sir?'

'David' he replies unable to keep still as he tries to keep the pressure off his bottom.

'So what seems to be the problem then David?' Billy asks; looking at the restless gentleman who's now leaning towards the other side of the armchair.

'Oh it's so...so painful' David replies. 'I woke up needing a poo and since then it's been very runny and there's blood coming out with it, I'm going every few minutes.'

'David can I check' Billy pauses as he gets interrupted by David leaning further away from him and lifting his bottom further off the armchair. 'Your blood pressure David, are you able to keep still while I check it?' Billy says finishing off his sentence.

'Oh yes go ahead, don't mind me lads, oh...Oh, it's getting uncomfortable again' David replies as he continues to move about on the armchair.

Billy just about manages to get a BP reading before David hastily interrupts.

'Oh I'm sorry lads I've gotta go again there's more.' He starts to get up just as Billy's about to remove the stethoscope from under the blood pressure cuff. Billy's ears get yanked forward with David's arm as he gets up quivering 'oh no...Oh no...' and quickly rushes off to the toilet with legs pressed tightly together. 'Oh lads I'm so, so sorry,' can be heard in the distance from the toilet up stairs.

'His BP's 136/80' Billy tells Mac as he rubs his sore ears.

'Aye that's good this one's all yours then laddie,' he replies with a smile.

 A few minutes later and David reappears with a temporary look of relief on his face.

'Oh that's a relief, sorry about that lads,' David says apologising.

'No need to apologise David' Mac tells him. 'But maybe it'll be a good idea to take some extra breeks with you, just to be on the safe side' he suggests as he then makes his way out to 0642 to prepare the trolley with a sheet and a few incontinence pads just in case.

'Do you feel ok to walk out to the ambulance?' Billy asks.

'Oh yes it feels much better when I'm standing, much better.'

Billy holds onto David's arm for support as they walk out to 0642. An apprehensive look fills David's face as his legs squeeze tightly together while making his way to the vehicle.

'Try to get your bahooky comfortable on here fella' Mac says pointing to the trolley.

David gently sits down and tries to get comfortable. Mac leans over trying to put the BP cuff back on his arm, but unable to get comfortable for long David's moving again; leaning over to the other side. Again he tries to put the cuff on, but David's shifting once more again, so standing still with the cuff in his hand Mac gives David a moment. Looking as if David's now as comfortable as he'll be Mac asks: 'Ye ok for me to put this back on now fella?'

'Oh yes go ahead, don't mind me' he answers back with an apprehensive look on his face.

Taking the ePCR of its docking station, Billy sits down opens the laptop up and logs on to start typing in David's details.

'Nae...McDamnock don't use the electronic handbag Willie, can't beat a bit of old fashioned pen and paper.' Not being one for change he despises the mini laptop.

'Here use the paperwork' Mac insists as he passes the pack of PRF's from the draw. After spending a few minutes going through the paperwork with Billy he checks David's BP again. 'You ok there David?'

'I'm ok for now just a bit sore down below, nothings coming out at the moment lads' David informatively replies.

Content the second BP is ok and not dropping, Mac smiles. 'Give us a shout when you're ready Willie' as he pats Billy on the shoulder before getting out and going round to the cab to get in the driving seat. As he puts his seatbelt on he hears from the back 'Oh I'm so sorry lads there's more coming' as a rather flustered Billy tries to comfort David the best he can. *'I feel for you* laddie' Mac says to himself. *'We've all been through it'* he adds as he leans over to the glove box and looks for a CD to put on.

Finally Billy peers through into the front. Covering his mouth and nose he coughs on the pungent aroma that's beginning to fill the back of the ambulance. 'I think we're ready to go now...Thanks mate' he says with a hint of sarcasm in his voice.

'Aye laddie, keep up the brave face' Mac replies with a smile as he spots a CD by Alabama 3. *'Aye that'll do'* he thinks to himself as he puts it in and turns up the volume before heading off to Casildon General.

All the way there he provides a slow, steady and smooth ride for the patient and of course his crewmate, while listening to the sounds of *'Too sick to pray'* coming from the CD player. Every now and then turning it down to hear David say 'oh I'm sorry lads there's more, oh I'm sorry' to which Mac would shout to his crewmate, 'you're doing a grand job laddie' but with no windows to open and the extractor fan not holding up to its name Billy's not impressed with Mac's words of support.

Arriving at A&E Mac opens the back door while whistling away to himself. David's still looking uncomfortable and still repeatedly apologising for the smell. 'Oh I'm sorry lads, I'm so sorry' while Billy's sat there pale faced.

'You're looking a wee bit peely wally Willie' Mac says.

'I'm fine, just fine' Billy replies trying not to take a deep breath in.

Mac then looks over at their patient. 'David don't keep apologising fella, there's no need...How's me lad been doing? Has he looked after you?'

'Oh yes he's been good putting up with me.'

Billy starts to look a bit worried that McDamnock's gonna just stand there and have a conversation, instead of getting the tail-lift down so they can get out of the ambulance. Discretely he tries to hint 'can we just get on with it.'

Mac looks at Billy all confused, his eyebrows move inwards as he tries to understand what Billy's attempting to suggest, before finally realising. 'Oh aye laddie of course.'

Unfortunately in A&E there's a delay before the nurse comes over to take a handover, which means a now all too familiar smell that Billy's still unadjusted to permeates through the corridor in A&E. *'But on the bright side'* thinks Billy. *'It gives me more time to go over my handover.'* While he finalises his handover in his mind Mac stands nearby, but not too near, his arms folded behind his back as he looks around unfazed by the aroma; still whistling the new tune stuck in his mind from the CD.

Eventually the nurse comes over apologising for the delay, but begins coughing as soon as the smell hits her.

'Oh I'm so sorry about that' David says continuing to apologise.

'David, no need to apologise' Mac repeats to him again.

'This is David' Billy tells the nurse in charge. 'He's been having a post rectal bleed this morning every time he has his bowels open...There's no abdo pain, his blood pressure's maintained and he's not hypotensive' Billy just manages to get out in one breath.

'Ok cubicle sixteen please,' she replies as Billy's facial expression now shows his anxiousness to move to another space for some fresh air.

In cubicle sixteen they help David slide over onto the hospital trolley while an amused McDamnock looks at Billy's face trying hard not to let the smell faze him.

'Take care David' Billy says, hoping David doesn't start a long conversation while trying not to make it look obvious he wants to leave the cubicle.

'Oh thank you lads, I'm so sorry about that,' David replies appreciating their help.

'No need to be sorry David, don't worry, hope everything's ok for you' Mac tells him.

Closing the curtain behind, Billy takes a deep breath and shakes his head trying to clear his nasal passages of the smell.

'Aye, well done Willie you kept it together' an impressed McDamnock tells him before heading back to 0642 with the trolley, whistling away again as he goes, leaving Billy still trying to regain his sense of smell as he makes his way out to reception.

Chapter 1.

'Who do you think you are? James Bond.'

The rest of the morning and into the afternoon carried on relentless, with an abdo pain *'can't be doing much with them laddie. A quick palpate then off to A&E, there's too many beasties in there for us to deal with.'*   An RTC where Mac tells Billy on route 'most of these are wee shunts, all minor injuries up and out prior us getting there.' But then says sternly 'McDamnock TC doesn't tolerate those that call 999 for whip-cash claims.'

By mid afternoon they've arrived back at Casildon General again with a catheter problem. 'Aye the folk of Casildon even think we can sort those blocked tubes out, but cannae be done by us we don't poke about down there. Unless a district nurse can perform their magic, A&E's where they have to go.' So after a bit of a delay waiting to off load as A&E's now full to the brim, they're ready to go.

'Is it always this busy?' Billy asks.

'Oh aye, there's no such thing as waiting around for the next job to come through, but that's what the folk think we do.'

The radio goes off in response to Billy's cell call request. '0642 green Casildon' Billy tells dispatch.

'Roger 0642, we're getting a pre alert for a job at the docks, details on their way.'

As they make their way towards the port the only details they have are for a male in his fifties fallen. Eventually more details come through at the same time dispatch call them up. 'Sorry for the delay 0642 details still sketchy, but looks like it's a car gone off the edge of the dock, unknown if the driver is out of the car. Helimed's running, HART are responding and a manager is on his way, but looks like you're closest still, so if you can give us an early update please, thanks 0642.'

'Looks like you could have something to get ya teeth stuck into Willie' Mac excitedly tells his crewmate.

'Well, going from nearly getting bitten and having my arse prodded by a dog, to losing my sense of smell, followed by getting wet on my first shift wasn't quite what I had imagined would happen on a first day.'

'Aye laddie, there's no other job like it.'

Arriving at the security gate for the docks, the port Police escort them through and on-towards berth thirteen.

'Hope you've brought your trunks Willie' Mac humorously tells him.

'Oh yeh, I'll be right behind my mentor...All the way' Billy wittily replies.

Turning into Berth thirteen everything looks as normal, no indication of an accident or incident having occurred. No group of people standing around by the edge of the dock looking worried. The port escort leads them to a group of workers gathered by a HGV car transporter. Getting out Billy gets the grab bag while Mac makes his way over to them.

As Billy reaches them, he hears his crewmate start talking to dispatch regarding the early update they requested.

'Naught sex for two here, ye can cancel Helimed, HART and the manager, the patient's out of the water, he's sitting on the dock of the bay. Get it Willie, dock of the bay like the song laddie' Mac says looking over at his crewmate finding his own sentence funny.

'Roger 0642, I'll stand down the other resources and leave you dealing, thanks for the update.'

Putting the grab bag on the floor, it's not hard to tell which one of the workers gathered is the patient, as the only one sat down is a fifty year old male with his clothes soaked through. He sits shivering as he grasps tightly a mug of tea and sips from it. One of his colleagues explains to Billy what happened.

'Well all I saw was Frank here, reverse off the trailer and drive forward, only instead of going slowly as he's close to the water' he says pointing in the direction of the dock's edge. 'He shot forward and straight off the bay. It looked an amazing stunt, the way the car went off and straight under.

'How long was he under for?' Billy asks.

'Well three of us were getting our boots off to jump in, but fortunately the windows were down so within thirty seconds Frank was bobbing about on the surface. Scared the right Shite out of us mate you did' Frank's colleague tells him.

'How on earth did you manage to head straight into the drink fella' Mac asks.

'It's an automatic and I think my boot got stuck between the accelerator and brake' Frank embarrassingly answers.

'It ain't an auto now' one of his colleagues shouts out. A moment of awkward silence follows before a Police car arrives and an officer walks over. 'We've gotta report of a drowning.'

'Nae, no drowning here' Mac answers. 'Just Frank who's accidentally accelerated a wee bit too far.'

'Frank' Billy says. 'Let's get you on our vehicle and do a few checks.'

In the back of 0642 Frank's not even had time to sit down when the officer can't resist a joke or two at his expense. 'At least it's not raining today.'

'I don't think Frank would have noticed' Mac answers for him, as he puts several inco sheets down on the trolley before a wet Frank sits down.

37

'I just need to get a few details from you and I'll let you shoot off' the officer quips. 'What's your surname Frank?'

'Drive-Bottom.'

'That is an unusual one' the officer tells him.

'My forefathers used to drive cattle in the vales.'

'And now you drive cars into'

Mac butts in. 'I think Frank's self-esteem's sunk to his boots at the moment fella, don't think it needs dragging down any further,' he says feeling sorry for him.

'Err...Sorry Frank, I am known for my dry sense of humour...Lets crack on shall we, I don't mean to make waves over your incident.'

McDamnock shakes his head. 'This is gonna be painful' he quietly says to Billy.

Over the next few minutes while Billy checks Frank over, the officer avoids the temptation to dive in with any more sarcasm while taking his statement. 'Just a couple more questions Frank and we'll be home and dry.' Well almost avoids anymore. A knock on the back door and one of Frank's colleagues stands there with some clothing they've managed to gather for him to change into.

'Best get those dry clothes on Frank' Mac tells him. 'And get ya-self home for a wee Dram' that'll sort you right out fella.'

'Well I'm about done too' the officer adds as they let poor Frank go and get changed.

'There goes one unlucky sole Willie' Mac say as they stand at the back door and watch Frank with the officer making their way over to his colleagues. 'Not only has he had the day from hell, but he's had to deal with an officer who's got as much sympathy as he has charisma.'

'It'll take me a day or so to type up my report' the officer informs Frank as they're about to part ways. 'As you can imagine I'm swimming in paperwork' he utters unable to resist. 'But if I need to get hold of you I guess you'll be floating around for a couple of days' are his parting words as he makes his way back to his car.

'Come on Willie, let's get out of here. I've had as much humour as I can take for one day' Mac says as they make their way round to the cab.

'Mac don't forget to mind the edge as you drive off, we don't wanna fall in.'

'Oh you're so funny.'

They return at the end of their shift forty five minutes late.

'Well, what do you think of your first day with old McDamnock?'

'Err...well...Interesting...More than I expected, much more' Billy replies, wondering if Mac will understand what he really thinks of his first day with this over the top, energetic, too energetic at times, big man.

Walking into the station, there's a pot of tea waiting on the table in the messroom just brewed by Phil.

'Do either of you boys want one?' Phil asks who's just started a nightshift.

'Not for me Philly, Mrs McDamnock's got a stew waiting and if I don't get home soon it'll be more than the pot stewing.'

'What about you Billy.'

'I'm ok, I'd better get home too...I've gotta put dinner in the oven, my other half will be home later than me, but thanks.'

 The Night-crew who've been sat waiting for their return get up to take their radios.

'Well hello there handsome,' a female voice says as she takes the radio from Billy's hand.

'Err...Hi' an embarrassed Billy replies.

'Donna don't get any ideas, me boy's got a lassie back home' Mac tells her.

'Me? I don't know what you mean Mac,' Donna tells him in a poor attempt at an innocent voice.

'Pay no attention to my crewmate she's got all the mouth and gives the impression she's a man-eater, but her bark's worse than her bite...By the way I'm Bob,' he says to Billy.

'Hi Bob I'm Billy' he replies as they shake hands.

'Don't mean to spoil the party lassies, but you need a few things on the bus' Mac tells them. 'Oh and some inco pads too, we used them all.'

But before Donna has the chance to give a sarcastic response, the radio goes off as another job comes through. Donna's one-way audible conversation with Bob can be heard all the way out to 0642; even outside her distinctive vocals can be heard as she rants on about not having time to get out to the vehicle.

'Aye poor old Bob I don't know how he manages...He's certainly got some patience with that lass' Mac tells Billy. 'Come let me show you where the paperwork goes at the end of the shift. 'Gotta look after the manager, can't leave him too much to do or he'll blow a fuse. He can't cope with more than one thing to do at a time.'

As Mac's about to walk out the door he remembers he's still got the ambulance keys in his pocket. 'Shit don't wanna to be taking these home with me,' he says annoyed with himself knowing he'll get stick off Donna for it. He quickly walks out to the Ambulance and finds Donna sat there in the driving seat frantically looking all over the place for the keys, moaning away to herself about where Mac's put them.

'Nearly ended up being a twally me-self' Mac says to her, his eyebrows frowned as he puts the keys in the ignition for her. 'And don't you dare give me any sarcastic comments girly!'

Donna chuckles at him, 'I'm not keeping score Mac, but I think that makes us even now...You can't moan at me anymore for taking them home.'

Without replying Mac just frowns at her, turns around and walks off over to Billy who's putting his kit in his car. He's just about to speak when Donna drives past giving a blast of the sirens, raising two fingers up and poking her tongue out at Mac, just to wind him up even more.

'She's certainly a handful that lass' Mac says to Billy. 'Anyway you did good today Willie, you did good...See you tomorrow for another bonnie day' he says while getting in his Jag. Starting it up, a cloud of smoke fills the air where Billy's standing as Mac shoots off with a trail of smoke following behind.

Billy stands there, smiles and thinks to himself *'well maybe he's not that bad. True he's a little excitable, difficult to understand; maybe too full of energy and a bit loud, but other than that, yer I guess he's alright. But it's certainly gonna be an experience working with him for the next three months.'*

McDamnock summed up he gets in his car and with his first day out on the road finished without any dramas he drives home.

Chapter 2

'I've met the family now.'

Oh great, four o'clock in the morning. I've woken up too early again, thirty minutes before my alarm. They say it's because you're keen when you start a new job, which I am, but I'm still feeling tired. Well I've been out on the road now for over two weeks, very much still 'fresh paint or wet behind the ears' as newbie's are called.

Not had anything major to deal with yet. *'Dinnae be keen to rush into the blood and guts jobs Willie'* as my crewmate would say. *'Cut ye teeth on the bread and butter jobs first.'* It's all well and good learning the theory stuff, but training school doesn't prepare you for the real world as I've already learnt.

Even the simple things like knowing what to say to a patient or their family when you first walk in. Or what to write on the patient report form, keeping it brief, though not too brief, but then not writing a 'war and peace' style novel either. It all takes time to learn, as well as remembering the abbreviations. Mac's given me a list of those most frequently used, like c/o; complaining of, Abx; antibiotics and so on. It's there in my pocket, discretely coming out whilst writing the paperwork, or using the electronic tough book when Mac lets me have a go on it. *'Nae electronic handbag for McDamnock, can't beat a bit of paperwork,'* my old fashioned crewmate keeps reminding me. He doesn't like using it because it never works properly for him.

I'm beginning to feel more confident as each shift passes and more comfortable using the radio when talking to dispatch. No long awkward pauses or mumbling into the handset now. My patient assessment's getting better too, it's starting to flow a bit more naturally, but there's still a long way to go.

In the short time I've been at Casildon-On-The-Hill ambulance station I've 'met the family now' you could say. There's Phil Best who I met first, he's well liked by everyone, very polite and quietly spoken, I like him.

Paramedic Donna Natasha Vaughan: AKA the Rottweiler, you wouldn't want to mess with her. She's loud, mouthy and a chain smoker who's not afraid to tell it like it is. She scares the shit out of me when she goes off on one.

Then there's Kerry Brown, I'd put her in the same category as Donna, scary. She's a Para too very similar to Donna. Kerry speaks her mind too and doesn't hold back on the colourful language. They both started at the same time, were on the same training course in which both of them were a nightmare for the instructors and then some bright spark had the idea of sending them both to Casildon as their base station. They are as stubborn as each other and neither has decided to move on. You don't want to put them together on an ambulance, it happened once before and Mac had to prise them apart, before they tore into each other, even for the big man they were a test to his caber tossing strength.

Para Brett Wood and Technician Corinne Ham work as a crew, their shift pattern follows Para Fred Wicks and his crewmate Technician Brian Treece. They're all likeable. Both Fred and Brian are old timers, seems like they've both been there since day one. They now work on the other ambulance that runs for just ten hours during the day, no more nights for them.

Two more gentle old timers are Technicians Bob Ward and Keith Bird, both likable too and both of whom are representatives for different unions. They're very proactive in helping newbies like myself and have given me lots of advice. Both Bob and Keith have been given Donna and Kerry as crewmates to keep the peace, apparently that didn't go down well to start with, but they've all adjusted now and got used to each other.

Then there's Sue Berry, every time Mac and me back her up they end up bickering. But when she's not winding Mac up or being wound up by him she comes across as funny, though I don't think she realises it. I can't help smiling at her everytime she opens her mouth. She's got a bubbly personality, always happy, sees the positive in everything and doesn't let things faze her easily. She's also got a laugh that can be heard before she's even entered a room, so you always know when she's arrived for a shift.

And then there's my crewmate McDamnock TC, Mac as he's known. I asked Phil what the T C stands for and he said 'nobody knows for sure it's always been a mystery. And when I asked the man himself, he just said 'not even Mrs McDamnock calls me by any other name bar McDamnock TC.' Mrs McDamnock or Maggie as he occasionally calls her has been married to him for many years, apparently she's wanted to trim those bushy eyebrows of his for a long time, but he wouldn't let her get near them with a strimmer.

 The only one I've not met yet is the station manager, who's been away for the past few weeks, Dickie Willoby: AKA 'Willoby the Wobbler' accordingly to the other staff he's good at managing a trauma job, but lacks people skills and throws his dummy out of his pram if he gets stressed, ironic really for a manager. He's described as being tall with no hair, but has a big handlebar style moustache and eyes that stare at you while he's talking. They say he's in a world of his own most of the time, so I can't wait to meet him.

 So after laying there in bed unable to get back to sleep, I get up, shower and put my green uniform on. I give my fiancée Samantha a goodbye kiss, who mutters in her sleep 'bye luv' as I walk out the bedroom, then downstairs and leave the house for work.

I arrive at station to find no one's there except Willoby the Wobbler. There he is, matching his description perfectly.

'Hello fella who are you?' he says in a strange cheerful, but confused tone.

'I'm Billy' I reply.

'How long you been working here then?' he asks standing there with a bouncy movement on his feet every time he talks.

I look at him bewildered. *'Are his pants are too tight?'* I think before replying. 'I've been here for a couple of weeks now.'

'Oh who you working with then?'

'McDamnock' I reply thinking: 'A*nd you're a manager.'*

'Ah McDamnock, he's a good egg.' At that moment Mac's Jag roars into the yard and makes its usual sound effects before he gets out. As he walks in he spots Dickie has cornered me and engaged me in what he assumes will be a normal bizarre Wobbler conversation.

'Willie, will you give me a hand with me motor' he asks.

'I see you've met Willoby the Wobbler then' he tells me as we walk over to his car. 'Thought you might need a bit of rescuing from the dunderhead.'

'Thanks, is he always like that?'

'Oh Aye, he's one of a kind.'

We stand by his Jag for a while: Mac telling me about its history before we head back towards the station.

'Time for a McDamnock brew Willie' he says as we walk in, which is something that I've still not got used to yet. We pass the manager's office and hear Dickie muttering away to himself, moaning about something he's got to do today.

'Don't worry, he's the only one who understands him' Mac says.

A couple of minutes later and I've got a McDamnock special brew in hand, I stand by the notice board reading the latest memos, most covered in correction pen marks, after someone has spotted Dickie's spelling mistakes. Then as I hear the front door open, Sue Berry's laughter can be heard bellowing down the hall. She comes in the mess room and cheerfully greets us.

'What Phil not back yet?' she asks.

'Dickie said Phil went out on a job when he came in this morning about ten past five,' I tell her.

'Anything to get away from the Wobbler,' Mac adds chuckling to himself while sat adopting the usual position; reclined back, newspaper in hand and tea balancing on chest.

Sue makes herself comfortable and reads her book, while I sit back and watch the early morning news on TV, enjoying the rest while we can before the night crew return and the day's mayhem begins.

 Phil comes in thirty minutes past his finishing time, due to waiting over an hour for an ambulance to convey his patient. Then shortly after Phil returns, 0642 comes tearing into the yard.

F***ing and blinding, Kerry comes into the mess room followed by Keith, who's looking tired from Kerry's colourful language or rather complaining about their last job.

'Mary Chadwell again, for F*** sake! That's twice in one night she's apparently fallen over and can't get up, have you met her yet Billy?'

'Ermm...No, no I don't think I have' I reply while thinking how much I'm starting to find her scary riled up look more funny now.

'She's one of our regulars, an alcoholic psycho patient who's either calling 999 because she's on the floor drunk, or wanting to be taken to A&E cos she believes she's 'F***ing possessed again' and rambling on about '*I need to see a psych doctor now!*' Apart from that she's f***king lovely,' Kerry explains in her unique descriptive way.

'Shall I take your radio Kerry' I say to her offering my hand out; while thinking of how to get out of her line of fire. She yanks it out of its holder on her belt, waving it about for a moment while still ranting on, this time about how late she'll now be when she finally gets home to get her kids ready for school.

Eventually I manage to get my hand onto the radio to take it off her and make my excuse to go out to the ambulance where Mac and Keith are talking union stuff. And, as soon as I go to restock equipment used by the night crew, the radio goes off for our first job of the day and it's my turn to attend for the first half of the shift. I get into the passenger side while Mac jumps in the driving seat, saying 'Well Willie here we go again.'

He makes a quick adjustment to the seat and we're off out of the station and on our way to somewhere in Casildon-On-The-Hill and so begins another day working in the Ambulance service.

Chapter 2

Tally-ho Basil.

One fine afternoon in the Wings RAFA club the only three remaining ex servicemen; Squadron leader Don Horn, Flying officer Basil Dann and Pilot officer Ron Wells, were having drinks. They only meet in the Wings RAFA on Tuesday afternoons, Churchill's public house Wednesdays, Saturdays and Mondays and the Lancaster public house on Thursdays and Fridays.

On this particular occasion they had been regaling tales of their service days gone by, over a pint or two of Casildon's finest ales.

Basil gets up to go to the bar when he suddenly feels faint, goes a paler shade of the whitest of the white clouds he's ever flown through and starts sweating profusely.

'I say' Don says to Ron. 'Looks like Basil's bought it.'

They spring into action grabbing Basil from behind and plonking him straight back down on his seat. 'Basil old chap can you hear me?' Don shouts at him.

'Yes Don I'm still with you, but the rooms moving a bit too fast to keep up with.'

Fearing his blood pressure may be low and he may pass out at any moment; just like back in the day pulling Gs' in the aircraft, they tip the chair backwards on to the floor with Basil still sat in it.

'I haven't seen Basil in that position since bailing out of his Spitfire' Ron says,

'I think we should call those emergency chaps Don.'

'Don't move the patient' the voice on the line from the ambulance service tells them, so leaving Basil in his lying back position they decide to move all of the tables and chairs away to leave a clear space for the ambulance crew.

'I fear Basil's only done this to get out of paying for his round,' a concerned Ron says to the Squadron leader.

'Yes he has always had deep pockets and short arms,' Don replies.

'Indeed made flying with this chap terribly difficult' Ron answers back.

'Basil stay with us old chap' Don tells the flying officer. 'Help is on its way.'

'Those boys in green will soon be here dear friend and we'll have you levelled off shortly' Ron adds.

'What we got then Willie?' Mac asks as another job comes through on the Terrafix screen, just when they had nearly got back to station for a McDamnock brew.

'Elderly male collapsed in club it says' Billy tells him reading the details.

'In a club, what type laddie? 'Not a cardiac arrest in the lap dancers club again surly Willie.'

'Unfortunately no Mac...It says at the Wings RAFA club in the High Street.'

'Oh aye that's a grand old place, I've been there before...The regulars will tell you some tall tales believe me.'

As they make their way through the country lanes towards the High Street of Casildon-On-The-Hill, Billy sat in the attendant's seat crosses his legs one way, then the other.

'Willie what's a matter with you? Don't tell me you need a pee after that last job already.'

'Mac did you see the state of that toilet in the farmhouse we've just left? There was no way I was gonna p*** in that so called bathroom.'

'Laddie you can't mess-about when you need to go...You gotta go! Better keep em crossed Willie; we'll not have any wet patches in the front of my ambulance!'

As 0642 pulls up outside the RAFA club, Mac jumps out while Billy cautiously steps out keeping his legs tightly pressed together. Mac's greeted by the barmaid.

'Why thank you me bonnie lass' he says to her as she leads him in. 'Me Willie's on he's way, having a wee issue at the moment he is.'

Billy still needing the toilet walks in a few foot steps behind, after composing himself while getting the kit from the back of the ambulance. The barmaid leads Mac to the double doors leading into the saloon. 'Most kind of you lassie' Mac says as he opens the saloon doors.

Billy, who's now caught up, stands next to Mac as they look across the empty saloon floor. There at the other end of the room they see Basil still sat on his upturned seat lying on his back.

'That looks a bit strange Mac.'

'Nae lad...I've seen stranger than that.'

'I say chaps over here' Don calls out to them. They quickly walk over and Billy aware he still needs the toilet cautiously kneels down on the floor next to Basil.

'Hello sir' he says with his head tilted sideways to be level with Basil's. 'What's your name?'

'Flying officer Basil Dann,' he replies looking up at him. Billy talks to Basil asking how he ended up in that position on the floor, as he does he takes Basil's blood pressure, while Mac clocks the Squadron leader's moustache.

'Aye that's some bonnie facial hair you have going on sir.'

'Awfully kind of you to notice sir' he replies. 'British moustache champion 3 years running…I'm Squadron leader Don Horn, pleased to meet you and that's a pair of impressive eyebrows you have there too Sir.'

An impressed McDamnock raises them in recognition. 'Aye…McDamnock TC's me name.'

'His BP's a bit low Mac' Billy says.

Mac looks over at Basil lying on the floor. 'You still look a wee peelie wallie Basil…last time I saw someone with that complexion was Willie on his first day' he says as he chuckles to himself. 'We can't get you up just yet or you'll be dropping down as soon as we let go…So we'll whip that chair out and elevate your legs up on some cushions for a while.'

Mac and Billy support Basil, while Don slowly slides the chair out from underneath. Basil lays there legs propped up by cushions, while Billy starts checking him over.

'That's it Willie get stuck in, its good practise for ya' Mac says as he gets a guided tour by Don of all the old framed photos on the walls. Each wall's covered in them; proudly displaying the servicemen that have long gone either standing by or sat in their flying machines of long ago.

'Always fancied the forces mee self, but dinnae get round to it' Mac tells him.

As the two carry on their photo tour, Billy still 'getting stuck in' continues checking Basil over, taking a small amount of blood from his fingertip to check his blood sugar levels, checks his temperature and then does an ECG.

As Don carries on giving Mac the low down on the history of every photo on every wall, Mac keeps a watchful eye on his young apprentice.

'How you getting on Willie?'

'All ok at the moment Mac, I'll soon let you know if anything changes.'

'You carry on then son' he replies.

After five more minutes and another blood pressure check Basil's BP is finally going the right way.

'It's up to 115/78 now Mac.'

'Aye that's better laddie' Mac answers back, just as he's being shown the last of the photos which just happens to be one of the three pilots sat in the RAFA a few years earlier.

He walks back over to Basil and Billy. 'I see there's more colour in those cheeks now young man' Mac tells Basil. 'Let's sit you up then, you can only lie on floor looking up at the ceiling for so long before it becomes boring.'

Slowly sitting up Basil says 'I say that's better now, you all looked a tad scary from down there.'

'You're not getting out of going to the bar Basil' Don reminds him. 'Just because you hit the deck, it's still your round.'

'Young man; I don't think there should be anymore ale for you today! Not unless you wanna end up on the floor again' Mac insists as the two of them help Basil to his feet. They let him sit on the chair for a few minutes though this time the right way up, before allowing Basil to stand.

'How's that feel?' Billy asks as they allow Basil to stand up on his feet.

'Oh yes much better I'd say...The rooms not moving around anymore.'

'Well if you feel back to normal now' Billy tells him. 'It looks like you've had syncope, a single faint.'

'Think a wee bit too much Casildon ale be the cause of that Basil?' Mac suggests.

The other two former pilots look away, mumbling under their breath 'who's a lightweight then...Who can't handle their ale.'

'So if you're content you're back to your normal flying officer's self' Mac continues. 'Then maybe one of these gentlemen will escort you home?'

'Oh yes I feel ready to get back in the cockpit' Basil tells Mac. And just as he mentions that, the other two start getting excited at the thought of being behind the controls with joystick in hand once more.

'Steady on boys, steady on' Mac tell the three grown men acting like excited children. 'Now this bit's important for you chaps so pay attention...Basil, you need to go straight home no more sorties at the bar you understand?..And it's your colleagues' mission, to get you a safe landing back indoors, you got that?'

'Yes Sir' the three of them reply while saluting Mac.

'Right then, we'll give you a copy of our paperwork and if you have any more low flying episodes or are suddenly taken unwell Basil, call our twallys back on 999 you got that?' Mac tells him.

'Roger that Sir, understood' he replies.

Mac finishes the paperwork, gives Basil a copy then they collect their equipment together and make their way back out of the club, leaving the three pilots to get ready to go home after another successful mission in the RAFA.

'I'm gonna need to relieve my bladder now' Billy tells Mac as he spots the toilet in the entrance hall. He passes the grab bag to him and quickly diverts in the direction of the toilet.

Sitting back in the cab again now feeling much better, Billy calls up despatch and informs them '0642 now green on scene...Patient recovered...Content to go home...Patient left in care of colleagues.'

'Roger 0642...You may return' comes the reply.

Just as they drive off they glance back in through the windows of the RAFA to see Basil back at the bar and another three pints sat on the table as he's handing over cash to the barmaid.

'Argh you see that Willie, that's three stubborn pilots back there for you. If he's not careful, it'll be Tally-ho- Basil!

Chapter 2

Some cardiac arrests you'll never forget.

It's the middle of a hot sunny afternoon and Mac and Billy are returning back to station. Mac's telling Billy about his days entering the tossing the caber competitions in the Highland games and how every morning he'll stand by the mantelpiece with a McDamnock brew in hand, admiring his tosser's trophies,

'Aye laddie five times champion I was' he says proudly. 'Sometimes I'll even ponder over who I'd award a tosser's trophy to within the ambulance service if old Mac were to give one away' he says with a grin.

They're nearly back to station for a chance to have one of those McDamnock brew's when a job comes through on the Terrafix:

'68 year old male collapse in car at Casildon Park woods' Billy says.

En-route to the incident, Billy whose confidence is growing each day, thinks about what he'll need to do when they arrive on scene, when an update comes through: *Patient now in cardiac arrest, you are sole response, no nearer vehicles available.*

Billy's face goes pale again, although he's attended an arrest before, that time was different. That time they were backing up a car, this time they'll be first on scene.

'Willie you're looking a bit peelie wallie again' Mac says looking at him. 'You'll be fine with old Mac by your side.'

He runs through some of the things they will do when they get there to try and help Billy's nerves. 'You grab the trolley Willie; we'll get him straight out and onto it, can't be doing CPR sat in a car. Then you concentrate on CPR and I'll do the running around you, getting on with the Para stuff.'

Going through Casildon High Street blue lights flashing sirens blaring away, they approach a zebra crossing to find an old lady starting to cross. Mac slams on the brakes and pulls up to the crossing. Lights still flashing, but not going anywhere he turns the sirens off.

'She ain't gonna stop she's goin all the way Willie to the other side.'

'Give her a break Mac she's probably got a hearing impairment' Billy says.

As she reaches the other side of the road she stops, looks at them and gives them a finger in the air sign. Then slowly turns back around and walks off.

'Hearing impairment...Really' Mac says with a frowned expression as he looks over at Billy before he puts his foot down again. Sirens back on, they speed away.

Arriving at the entrance to the woods, they're met by a member of the public who leads the way to the location. She guides them through the main car park and further into the wooded area which becomes quieter and more secluded. Up ahead they see the patient's car with a female in her sixties all dressed up, sporting a big hair do and face caked in makeup, but looking a little dishevelled as she stands next to the car with a worried look on her face.

Mac slams on the brakes and 0642 slides on the gravel before coming to a halt. As they pull up next to the car; a cloud of dust drifts across the woman. Mac gets the grab bag while Billy goes round and opens 0642's back door. He nervously lowers the tail-lift and grabs the trolley. His heartbeat now racing as he waits for the trolley to be lowered down on the tail-lift. Once on the ground he struggles to get the trolley to grip on the gravel as he tries to steer it towards Mac.

Finally he gets to the car and sees the patient; he's approx 16 stone and sat reclined in the driver's seat. Shirt unbuttoned, trousers undone, his face looks purple and lifeless with his arms flopped down by his side as Mac attempts CPR in such an awkward position while waiting for Billy.

'How long's he been like this lass' Mac asks the woman.

'Only a few minutes before I called' she replies. 'He was talking to me up till then.'

Mac frowns as he ponders over that for a moment, but no time to go into further discussion now Billy's here with the trolley. Mac positions himself beside the patient's upper body while Billy grabs hold underneath the patient's legs. For a brief moment a bizarre scenario ensues as they struggle to lift the patient out of the car, both looking like they're dancing with the patient. They shuffle this way and that as they try to manoeuvre towards the trolley. This made all the more difficult by the fact that the patient's unfastened trousers are now falling down.

'Willie his breeks are on their way down' Mac shouts.

'I know, I know' comes his reply as Billy's back nearly gives way.

With a groan and sigh of relief they place the patient ungracefully down on to the trolley. Billy tries to continue CPR in between helping Mac steer the trolley back onto the tailift and up and into the ambulance. Billy already feels knackered after just transferring the patient to the ambulance, but knows there's no time to pause.

Now standing at the head end of the trolley Billy continues CPR as Mac's gained IV access in the back of the patient's hand. While performing CPR Billy can't help but look forward and notice the patient's leopard skin patterned pants; which became exposed while lifting the patient out of the car. No matter how much he tries to ignore them; his eyes are drawn back to this underwear garment that would seem out of place on any elderly gentlemen other than Rod Stewart or Peter Stringfellow. As the patient's body wobbles with each chest compression, he begins to think this is gonna be one of those images that will haunt him forever.

With the first dose of adrenaline given, they swap places so Mac can intubate the patient; inserting a tube into his airway. Billy's now standing at the side of the trolley continuing with chest compressions and trying hard to keep the 70's style undergarment out of his view.

'Aye there she goes' Mac says as the tube's inserted into the trachea and secured. Connecting it to the ventilator; it begins to make a deflating squeaky balloon sound as the patient's lungs inflate automatically with oxygen. Pausing for a moment Mac looks over at his crewmate. 'Willie how you doin...You ok?'

'I'm ok' he replies red faced, sweat now pouring down his face.

'You're doing a belter of a job laddie...You just need to grow some eyebrows like mine to stop the wee bits of sweat dripping down into your eyes' he says wiping his crewmate's forehead with some paper towel.

Second five minute check on the patient's heart rhythm and it's still asystole (flat line). Mac then takes over chest compressions to give Billy a breather. They swap over again two minutes later; Billy back on the chest. Then pausing for a third rhythm check; it now shows a slow rhythm as Mac feels a weak pulse in the patient's neck. 'He's gotta wee pulse, but it's too slow...Probably just the Adrenaline, but we'll be here all day waiting to see any further improvement. Let's give some Atropine and get going laddie 'he says wiping the sweat off his crewmate's forehead again.

Atropine drawn up and a 500mcg dose given Mac takes over chest compressions as the half dose has not improved the patient's cardiac output. Billy gets out the back and shuts the door. As he does; standing the other side of it is the woman.

'JESUS!' he says loud as her dishevelled looking hairdo and makeup gives him a fright.

'Can I come with you' she asks. 'I don't live around here you see?'

'Erm... ok, but it's probably best if you sit in the front with me.'

Seat belts on; Billy waits for the go ahead to set off to the hospital. Mac wedges himself in a standing position with one leg against the trolley and the other against the attendant seat opposite so he can continue chest compressions; as the patient's pulse is still too slow to sufficiently pump enough oxygenated blood to the brain.

'Willie off you go and can ya put an alert call in to Casildon for me?' he shouts through to the front as he continues CPR.

'Will do Mac.' Using the vehicle's radio he calls up Casildon General on the alert line, before gently pushing down on the accelerator as he turns the ambulance around and cautiously makes his way back out of the woods over the rough ground.

'Casildon A&E' the voice over the hands free speaker answers.

Billy gives them the information while trying to keep the vehicle movement smooth over the uneven terrain.

'Male, approx seventy years of age.

Cardiac arrest.

Weak carotid pulse, but less than 10 per minute. Intubated and drugs given.

ETA about twenty minutes.

'See you in resus,' the voice replies.

To try and make the atmosphere between him and the woman in the front a bit less tense, Billy switches on the radio and the CD player starts to play loudly. Accidently the volume had been left turned up as the Alabama 3 CD Mac put in before booms out a track called 'In the presence of the Lord.' Billy quickly leans over to the centre of the dash to turn off the inappropriate music. With one hand he fumbles at the radio controls while the other steers

59

the vehicle, trying to keep the drive as smooth as possible for Mac in the back. Unfortunately he hits the radio function button instead and 'Another one bites the dust' by Queen now booms out of the speakers. But, as they're at the entrance to the main road the volume has to wait as Billy needs both hands on the wheel. Once on the straight and smoother main road with the inappropriate sounds of Queen's hit song blasting out; Billy quickly turns the radio off. 'Sorry about that' he says embarrassed.

As 0642 drives along with its lights flashing and sirens howling through the quiet afternoon countryside towards Casildon General. Billy's itching to turn the radio back on to ease the quietness in the front, but decides not to in-case an inappropriate song blasts out of the speakers again, so deciding against risking that he starts a conversation instead.

'So where do you live?' he asks. Suddenly the woman bursts out crying. 'Oh I'm sorry' Billy says and thinks *'bad idea then.'* He decides it's best to just concentrate on getting to the hospital.

 After twenty one minutes of driving, listening to the sound of the ventilator, sirens and occasional noise from Mac as he's shoved from side to side, they arrive at Casildon General. Billy pulls up in the ambulance bay right outside the entrance to resus.

'If you wait here I'll take you into the relative's room in a minute' he says to the woman.

Jumping out the vehicle he runs around to the open the back doors. Inside there's Mac with sweat running down his forehead and around his eyebrows as he continues chest compressions; the second dose of Atropine didn't work. Two nurses from resus come out to meet them, one escorts the female into the relative's room while the other helps them take the trolley off the vehicle and rush into resus. They slide the patient over onto a hospital trolley and the nurses take over chest compressions. Then like an announcer on stage waiting for the audience's attention, Mac waits till all the doctors are looking at him. 'Don't do a handover in resus Willie till you've got everyone's attention' he whispers to Billy. Then when there's quiet in the room and all the doctors eyes are on him, he begins; that unmistakable Scottish accent booming across the trolley.

'Approx age of male Seventy years, collapsed in car.

In asystole on arrival.

Eight adrenaline and 1mg Atropine given altogether.

Has had a weak carotid pulse, but remained less than 10 beats a min.

Past medical history unknown.

Cause of arrest...You can ask the lass that's came with him about that one.'

The motionless doctors hanging onto everyone of Mac's words suddenly spring into action giving their orders to the nurses and starting to take bloods from the patient.

'How was that Willie?'

'Beautiful Mac...beautiful. I'm sure as fine-a-handover as you've ever given' Billy replies as they stand there for a minute watching the doctors and nurses now perform.

Billy grabs the trolley and takes it out of resus, passing Mac on the way out he sees him standing next to a clinical waste bin taking his gloves off. After an hour of wearing that non latex protective wear; his fingers finally see the light again as sweat pours out of the gloves.

'Hey Willie feast your eyes on the hard work coming out of these beasties' he exclaims.

Hands now washed Mac goes out to reception to book the patient in before returning to 0642 and finally getting a chance to sit down, but not to rest as he's still gotta do the paperwork. Passing the back of the ambulance he sees

Billy clearing up the mess he left. 'Sorry laddie, but it's not a proper job unless it looks trashed in the back' he tells Billy.

Paperwork finally complete Billy follows Mac back into resus to hand over his paperwork. The cubicle they took the patient into now has the curtains closed. They stand outside as Mac quietly says to Billy 'We do all that hard work Willie and these give up after a wee five minutes effort.'

'Sorry Mac' the Doc says walking over. 'But we ain't Gods...The pulse had gone again by the time you left resus and he's been down far too long. Over an hour now and with no sign of improvement you know that's a non-viable resus,' the Doc adds before walking off.

'Aye Doc I know,' Mac replies looking at the closed cubicle.

'So that's it' Billy asks confused. 'We do all that and when we get here it's over just like that.'

'Aye me lad, it's a tough world at times no matter how much we may do out there, but as the Doc says they ain't gods.'

Just then a shriek could be heard from behind the curtain as a nurse comes out looking flustered.

'Well that's embarrassing' she says. 'So I'm cleaning him up and there's all these wet tissues stuffed in his pockets and lipstick round his manhood...Yuk' she says shuddering as she walks off.

Another nurse walks in from the relative's room.

'Mac how long did you say it was before she called for help?...As she's just told me she had to make herself look presentable first and couldn't give me an exact time on how long it was before calling 999.

'Well she obviously had her hands full' replies Mac, then he frowns realising his own sentence may have come out wrong.

'Well I gave her the bad news that he's passed away and she asks me *'have we gotta tell his wife? Cos my husband doesn't know about us either'...* 'apparently they've been at it for over twenty five years.'

Bemused, Mac's eyebrows rise. 'He may have gone with a smile Willie, but what a bloody mess he's left behind. Lesson there for you there laddie, don't go putting it about no matter what age you are.'

Chapter 2

The AA incident

It's a summer's evening in Casildon-on-the-Hill, an Alcoholics Anonymous meeting is being held in the local village hall. The atmosphere is hot, humid & sweltering with every seat taken. The speaker Leslie Love is talking to the good people of Casildon, they listen attentively to the fine upstanding gentleman they all look up-to for help when in need. As he tells them how well they're all doing and not to let that devil alcohol back into their good lives, a lady in her fifties suddenly stands up shouting;

'I can't breathe help me, I can't breathe' and then collapses to the floor.

The congregation gasp and gather around her trying to help, but instead make the atmosphere even hotter as she lays there swamped by them all.

'It's Margaret, Margaret Tring' says a voice from the congregation.

'Margaret are you ok?' the worried voice asks.

'I can't breathe,' she dramatically replies grabbing hold of the worried member's clothing 'I can't breathe.'

One of the congregation screams 'Call for the Paramedics!'

Leslie comes over to the lady on the floor where everyone has gathered and decides that the crowd is only making things worse.

'Calm down everybody, calm down' he says to the congregation. 'Please give this lady some space.'

They move back...Slightly, all still wanting to see what is going on. They chatter nervously as they wait for the ambulance. Their wait seems to go on and on as they wonder how it can take so long to arrive as the ambulance station is only across the road. Unfortunately the good people of Casildon don't realise there hasn't been an ambulance on station all day. They're out attending to patient's around the clock, the Casildon folk don't realise that the Ambulance service is stretched beyond its capacity due to the excessive demand on it.

Gradually a familiar sound of sirens can be heard, distant at first but becoming louder and louder as the ambulance gets closer. The congregation look at each other in anticipation as Margaret lies on the floor still saying in dramatic tone 'I can't breathe,' as she grabs hold of Leslie's shirt.

In a cloud of dust the ambulance screeches to a halt outside, blue flashing lights shining through the windows. The noise of doors opening & closing from outside can be heard, followed by footsteps on the gravel marching up to the entrance. The doors to the village hall fly open and with sunlight raging through, the only shade is provided by the shadows of McDamnock & Billy as they stand at the entrance, grab bags in hand.

Then that Scottish voice booms out into the hall;

'Did somebody call for an Ambulance?'

For a moment silence fills the air, the congregation stand to attention as if a Headmaster has spoken. Then a voice calls out;

'Yes...Please over here, come quickly she can't breathe' cries the voice from among the crowd.

The two march over to the scene, the congregation parts as Mac and Billy make their way through. Mac kneels down beside the patient.

'Lassie, tell me what's wrong.'

'I can't breathe, I can't breathe' she answers back as she latches onto him.

'Lassie your breathings sounds fine to me or you wouldn't be telling me that,' Mac says as he loosens her grip on him...'Now tell me lassie, what's your name?'

'It's Ma....' It's Ma....' she stutters trying to get her name out in one breath.

'Mabel?' Mac asks.

'No' its Ma....' she tries again to get her name out.

'Madge...Is it Madge?'

'No...It's...' Is as far as she can say, unable to say a full sentence.

'Maisie?'

She shakes her head, unable to catch her breath.

'Mavis?' Mac asks looking baffled now he's running out of names to ask.

She shakes her head again now looking frustrated. Billy leans over to one of the congregation and asks;

'Do you know this lady?'

'Oh yes its Margaret' two of them reply at the same time.

Looking back at Mac, Billy does a double take at the two ladies; wondering *'Why didn't they just say that in the first place when we asked Margaret.'*

Mac looks at their patient. 'Margaret your breathing is a wee bit fast, now you need to slow it down...Slow it down, that's it focus on me and we'll soon have it under control.' Mac Coaches Margaret to slow her breathing down. 'In through your nose lassie, out through your mouth...In through your nose and out through your mouth...In, out...In, out...Aye Margaret that's it.' As she follows his commands she can't help but focus on Mac's eyebrows. Up and down they move in time with his coaching words 'in and out.'

Following this breathing technique Margaret becomes more & more hypnotised by their movement and before long her breathing is in sync with Mac's eyebrows. Then while still mesmerised by them she sighs and with a smile says;

'Ah that's better, I can breathe.'

The crowd applaud as they think the big man with the eyebrows has cured Margaret. Then as the sound of clapping dies down a crashing noise from the other side of the hall can be heard.

The crowd part again allowing Mac to look past them in the direction from where the noise came. His eyebrows give a stern McDamnock look towards the new incident that's occurring. A member of the congregation who had been sleeping throughout has fallen off her chair. Legs akimbo on the upturned piece of furniture she's now awake and starts to emit a soft moan.

'Oh ignore her' says Leslie. 'That's just Mary Chadwell; she's always drunk when she attends and normally falls over once or twice before she leaves.'

Mac's eyebrows rise up for a moment giving a look of surprise; as the folk of Casildon never cease to amaze him.

'Margaret have you got any pain?' Mac asks.

'No sir I feel fine now' she says as she stares at Leslie.

'So tell me what happened then.'

'Well I remember feeling hot, very hot and getting even hotter. My breathing was getting heavier and heavier,' she explains in a dramatic tone.

'Aye lassie we got the drift' Mac says interrupting.

'And then' Margaret says with eyes open wide...There...There was nothing.'

Coughing to clear his throat after listening to Margaret's over the top story, Mac says;

'Margaret let's check your blood pressure shall we.'

While the blood pressure cuff tightens around her arm Billy asks;

'Do you have any problems with your blood pressure?'

'No I'm as fit as a fiddle' she replies.

'So you're not on any tablets for anything?' Billy enquires.

'Oh yes I take tablets for blood pressure, thyroid, diabetes, arthritis, anxiety...' Margaret explains as the list seems to go on.

'Lassie going by your very descriptive explanation I think you've had a wee panic attack from the hot atmosphere in here.'

'Really...A panic attack, sounds serious' she replies sounding surprised and excited. 'Wait till I tell everyone what I've had. I could have died.'

'Err...No lassie not a heart attack, a panic attack.'

'They all be jealous,' she replies totally unaware of what Mac's trying to explain.

'Tell you what lass; let's give you a check over in the ambulance shall we.'

'Thank you that would be lovely.'

'No worries lassie, if McDamnock can't fix you he'll send you on your way with a haggis.'

'Really' she replies believing this to be true as they help her off the floor.

'No of course not, I'm just jesting with you. You English think that's all us Scots eat, can't stand the stuff me-self.'

Once on her feet, they allow Margaret to get her balance and compose herself before walking out to the ambulance.

'Can I come in the ambulance too' Leslie asks. 'Margaret's a dear member of the congregation.'

'Aye of course' Mac replies.

The congregation wish words of kindness to Margaret as they pass them. 'Hope everything's ok' one says, followed by more comforting words. 'Hope you're alright.' 'Come back soon.' 'Yes come back soon...We want our Leslie back, don't be so selfish' another voice shouts from the back of the crowd.

Mac holds the door to the hall open as Billy leads Margaret and Leslie out and into the ambulance. As Mac closes it he notices the member of the congregation who'd fallen off her has got up and is now sat on her chair. Mary Chadwell looks around, totally unaware of all the excitement that's been going on.

In the ambulance Billy completes the rest of the checks while Mac fills the paperwork in.

'Margaret everything that we can do seems ok.' Billy tells her. 'So like my colleague said it looks as though it was just a panic attack. Have you had anything like that before?'

'Oh no I've never had an attack of anything before. Think I would have panicked if I did...But I got so very...very...very hot in there I couldn't breathe, couldn't breathe I say.'

'Aye lassie we got that bit' Mac says; thinking *'she can certainly talk for England whether she thinks she can breathe or not.'* 'Well I think you'll be ok now lassie.'

'Yes I think I'll be now, now that Leslie's here with me.' Margaret tells Mac. 'Leslie can take me home can't you dear' she says with a smile on her face.

Mac interrupts with a serious look on his face. 'Aye lass you need a cup of tea and put your feet up for a while, make sure to have plenty of fresh air and no getting hot-n-bothered for the rest of the evening, you get what McDamnock's saying?'

'I'll make sure my clothing is loose and I'll take a cool shower if I get hot' she replies while looking at Leslie.

'Hmm' Mac mumbles in a disapproval tone as he tears off a copy of his paperwork and passes it to her. 'Keep this with you in-case you have to call 999 again.'

'Thank you so much, you've both been very very kind' she replies as she puts the paperwork in Leslie's pocket.

'Ok Margaret all the best, but remember straight home now lassie' Mac insists as they let them out of the ambulance and on their way.

'That's good of Leslie to take her home' Billy says.

McDamnock chuckles and looks at him. 'Don't think he's taking the lassie home laddie, more like back to his house. Margaret and Leslie, they're the worst kept secret in Casildon; the only person who doesn't know about them is her husband.'

Chapter 2

'He was no boy scout Willie'

Not all the folk in Casildon-On-The-Hill are happy souls, sometimes life becomes too much to handle and some seek a way out. One such resident is Harry Hobbs always known as 'Happy Harry,' the owner of a local building firm with many years success, but the financial crisis of late has even hit some of Casildon's inhabitants. Harry's now on the verge of bankruptcy and become a manic depressive, he suffers with bipolar, been diagnosed schizophrenic and has episodes of paranoia since his wife left him for the postman.

For the past three weeks he's been at his lowest and contemplating ending it all, and has now come to the conclusion that the quickest way is to take himself to a field in his car with some rope, tie one end around his neck and the other around a fence post then drive off in order to kill himself, either from decapitation or asphyxiation.

The evening of Friday the thirteenth is the day he has decided he will carry out this horrific event. So, he drives towards the spot he has already chosen and as he does Harry begins to get nervous. With sweating palms; he grips the steering wheel tighter in order to concentrate and to stop him changing his mind, but instead he finds himself driving aimlessly around Casildon-On-The-Hill before arriving at the field, but it's a lot later than he anticipated, it's now dark.

 Getting out of the car he opens the boot and gets the rope out. He picks a post in the fence that separates two farmer's fields, ironically where he had built barns for both of those farmers many years ago. Unfortunately for Harry the section of fence he has chosen is damaged and weak, but as it's too dark Harry's unable to see this as he ties the rope around it.

Getting back into the car he puts the seat belt on then pauses for a moment, just staring into the darkness before putting the other end around his neck and tying it tightly. He revs the engine several times, his hands still sweating as he grips the steering wheel tighter than before. He takes a deep breath, swallows and puts the car into drive then presses his foot down hard on the accelerator. The car slides to the left as it tries to grip in the mud before moving forward and then sliding to the other side as it begins to accelerate along the field. As it gathers speed the slack rope laying on the ground gets shorter and shorter till there's none left and it pulls upwards. The tension between the end round Harry's neck and the other around the fence post only lasts a split second before the rope breaks in half, but not before the fence post comes hurtling out of the ground in the direction of Harry's car.

His neck jolts back into the seat from the tension, but then is jolted forward as the rope brakes. Harry's thinking this is it, he keeps his arms straight and foot flat to the floor on the accelerator, not realising the rope had snapped. Harry's driving as fast as he can make the car go. And go it does...Straight into a tree. The car comes to a halt followed by the fence post flying through the air and bouncing off the roof before landing on the ground next to it.

Harry sits motionless in his seat wondering if he's dead, but suddenly realises he's breathing loudly *'Damn it! it's not worked,'* he thinks to himself. He tries to turn his head, but begins to feel pain in his neck as soon as he tries to move. He clinches to the steering wheel, too afraid to move as he realises the rope pulling tightly around his neck may have done some damage.

Aware of something approaching in his peripheral vision from the left, he turns his eyes towards the figure to see a cow coming up to the car munching grass; right up to the car door it comes before it stops and stares at him. Realising he's stuck Harry begins to panic; his breathing quickens and becomes louder. Again he looks out the window towards his left at the cow still staring at him and chewing loudly; its large bottom jaw slides side to side as it crunches on the grass. Harry feeling helpless as he looks at the cow still staring back, realises he has only one option. In desperation he reaches for his mobile in his right trouser pocket and rings his ex wife. As she answers Harry nervously says 'Sue I've erm...erm...had a bit of an accident.'

'What do you mean accident?' she shouts back at him. 'Harry I hope you're not trying to make me feel guilty AGAIN.'

Not wanting to go into detail he just says 'Erm...I'm stuck in my car in a field off Lovers Lane, South Casildon. Please Sue, send someone to help.'

Reluctantly Sue calls 999 for the Fire brigade who in turn call the Ambulance control centre requesting an ambulance attends as there's a possibility the patient's injured.

'Naught sex four two green at Casildon,' Mac tells despatch as they are now ready to go again after the last job.

'Roger 0642 another job for you' comes the reply.

Reading the terrafix screen Mac's eyebrows meet in the middle of his forehead as he's bewildered by the details: *50 year old male, stuck in a car, in a field, possibly serious injuries. Police and Fire Brigade on route. Location: Field off of Lovers Lane South Casildon-On-the-Hill.*

'There's many a field in Lovers Lane lassie, do you have any more location details?' Mac asks despatch.

'Details came from Fire Brigade, caller's not with patient, but I'll get back to them and find out if they can get any more details on the location,' despatch answer back.

Mac then looks at Billy 'we're clinicians not magicians, this could end up a bit of a wild goose chase Willie,' as Billy drives off out of Casildon General again.

On the way Mac turns on the CD player, the Alabama 3 CD still inserted starts playing as 0642 makes its way out of Casildon-On-The-Hill and into the surrounding rural countryside. Blue lights flashing with the occasional blast of the tartan trumpet; they speed along to the 'Sounds of the loneliness' blaring out from inside the cab.

Arriving at Lovers Lane the satnav's directions stop as it indicates they've arrived on scene. But the 999 call wasn't made from the exact location of the patient and with the dim evening light fading fast the only way of finding the patient's car is with 0642's side mounted spot lights, flashing blue-lights and the vehicle's head lights. Travelling from west to east along Lovers Lane with the lights piercing through the darkness around them, they're joined by a Police car following behind, then a fire-engine turns up travelling in the opposite direction.

A couple of minutes later and 0642 can be seen travelling along the same stretch of road, this time from east to west and now passing the fire-engine again travelling in the opposite direction with the Police car now following behind the fire engine. 0642's radio goes off as despatch call, 'Apparently the patient is in a field with a broken wooden gate at the entrance.' Just then Billy slams on the brakes and reverses back.

'That looks like it Mac' he says pointing out of Mac's window and across the field.

'Aye Willie well spotted, that's some hawk eyes you've got there.'

They turn into the field and get out; proceeding on foot as the ground's too soft for the ambulance to venture any further forward. Shining a torch across the field McDamnock's light finds the car; its front is caved in up against a large tree.

Getting closer Billy says 'What's that cow doing there?' as it starts to stare at him.

'No idea Willie, but see if you can get it to mooo've... get it?' he says laughing.

'But I've no experience with cows Mac.'

'No me neither, but it's on your side of the path and she's staring at you laddie.'

While Billy cautiously goes over to the cow, Mac goes up to the car door and shines the torch through the window to see Harry sat frozen to the spot. He manages to open the damaged door. 'Well hello there fella, what you doin parked in a field with a cow?

'Wincing in pain, Harry tells Mac about the events leading up to this evening's drastic actions. Mac's attention flits between Harry's story and the sound of Billy trying to shift the cow. 'But that cow's nothing to do with me' Harry adds at the end of his tragic story.

'Aye money or a lassie, I knew there be one of em involved and I'm glad you say the cow's nothing to do with it...By the way I'm Mac and the wee lad around the other side playing with the cow is me crewmate Billy, what's your name?' Mac asks.

'It's...It's... Harry 'he exclaims feeling distressed and ashamed after opening up about everything and then starts breathing fast again. 'You must think I'm a thundering idiot for doing this' he says to Mac as he starts crying.

'We haven't come all the way out here to ridicule you Harry, no man; we're all 'a Jock Tamson's bairn's.'

Harry stops crying and his breathing slows down. 'Huh...' he replies confused.

'It means we're all God's children, nobody's better than anybody else-we're all equal' Mac softly explains to Harry. 'We can't have you sat there all night can we, we'll soon have you out. But, if your necks hurting when you try to move; unfortunately Harry we'll have to lay you flat on a spinal board, just in-case there's any damage to your neck so the Doc in A&E can give you the once over. The good news is that you haven't lost any feeling in your arms or legs so I'm sure you'll be sat up again in no time...But first, we'll have to get the 'water fairies' to make some alterations to your car, in other words the roofs gotta come off.' At that point Billy runs around to their side of the car puffing and panting away.

'She ain't moving Mac, she won't budge at all.'

'Right Willie you hold Harry's head nice and still while I'll go get a neck collar and board, but first I'll sort out the wee beastie for you.'

Mac goes over to the cow calling despatch on the way. 'We've found our patient now so let the Fire Brigade and Police know the location's where the gate is...Over' Then as he gets near to the cow he bends down level to the beast and stares her in the eye. 'Well Daisy it's either you or me and I don't fancy your chances.' Walking around to the side of the cow he slaps her on the rump and she trots off; just as the sound of sirens from the fire engine can be heard as it arrives at the gate closely followed by the Police. Mac shakes his head as he wanders over to 0642 whispering to himself *'why do they need to make so much noise this time of night, there's not even anyone else out here.'*

Once Mac's got a neck collar and the board from 0642 he makes his way back to the car, explaining to the leading fire and police officers about Harry's story. The Fire brigade then set up their equipment and flood lights soon begin to illuminate the scene. The sound of generators break the silence all around and the whole field now begins to resemble a film set. 'Willie get your helmet on cos you're going in the back to hold Harry's head' Mac tells him.

With Billy sat in the back seat of the car holding Harry's head still, Mac puts a collar around his their patient's neck and gets another set of observations done before the Fire brigade get stuck in. 'Your BP and pulse is up a wee bit Harry, but not surprising as you've got quite a party going on around you.'

Once Mac's out of the way; the Fire brigade start cutting the side pillars of the car with their *'jaws of life' AKA* hydraulic cutters. They lift the roof off like a lid off of a biscuit tin and then with full access to Harry's car Mac takes over immobilisation of Harry's head. 'Put a wee bit of faith in us Harry' he says as they recline his chair back and giving Billy the responsibility of commanding the firemen, they place the spinal board between the seat and Harry's back. Under Billy's commands they slide Harry up the board and then slide the board backwards until it rests on top of the newly converted open top car.

Billy places head blocks either side of Harry's head and then secures the straps around Him and the board. Utilising Casildon's 'burly fireman' they carry Harry on the board across the field to the Ambulance, though Mac would disagree with the term 'burly' as a description for the firemen. *'They'd be no match for me in a caber contest'* he thinks to himself.

Once inside the ambulance with the doors shut, Mac and Billy swap the board underneath Harry for the scoop; a less uncomfortable piece of equipment. Then set about more observations while the Police look through Harry's car just to make sure there's nothing else of concern about the events of this evening. In the boot they come across a bag with yet more spare rope in. After a knock is heard on 0642's back door Mac opens it and is called outside by the Police officer for a quick word. A few minutes later he gets back in. 'The Police will come and have a wee chat with you in A&E Harry...Just a welfare check, nothing to worry about. Right then Willie we ready to go then, I think Harry's been through enough tonight don't think you need to be on this scoop any longer than necessary.'

Billy's drive back to Casildon General is nice and smooth, minimal roll around the bends, smooth braking with a feathered touch to bring 0642 to a stop at every traffic light. His driving's come a long way since his first day out. Something that Mac's noticed as he peers through into the front to congratulate him on when they reach A&E. 'Very smooth drive Willie, very smooth.'

Once inside the General Billy takes note of how professional Mac's handover is, discreet and sensitive in giving Harry's story over to the major's nurse. Then into a cubicle they transfer Harry on the scoop over onto a hospital trolley.

'Now you look after yourself, you hear me Harry?' Mac tells him.

With a smile of gratitude Harry replies 'I will and thank you, both of you.'

Billy takes the trolley back to 0642 and Mac heads off to reception.

Getting back in the cab of 0642 Mac tells Billy what the policeman wanted to have a chat about while they were still on scene, telling Billy about a shopping carrier bag and spare rope they found in the boot of Harry's car. 'I think the reason Harry's still with us Willie is all down to the quality of rope...If he had bought a quality rope from anywhere else instead of Casildon Cash savers, he may not be with us now!'

Chapter 3

Getting to know thy regulars,

and yes, these really did occur

It's been two months since I started out on the road with Mac. I'm now feeling more settled in the role and have become used to and dare I say fond of the old man. I know he's Stubborn and set in his ways, but he's got a lot of experience and a big heart to go with it.

Mac used to ask the patient questions along with me, so there were no long awkward pauses while I stand there thinking *'what do I ask now?'* Or he'll prompt me to do something I'd forgotten to do. *'No awkward moments in front of your patient laddie, you work together, you learn together. There be plenty of time to go ahead on your own in the future.'* Slightly different to what I thought he was going to do to me on my first day, when he jokingly said he'll do the first job then it was all mine.

Now he stands back and lets me get on with it, waiting to be asked to do something. Usually I'll find him wandering around looking at photos or admiring paintings on the wall of a patient's home. He'd make it look like he was in a world of his own; standing there with his hands behind his back while staring at a painting and then remind me that he was still keeping an eye on me. *'Don't forget to ask the patient how to describe their pain laddie'* would come out of his mouth disguised amongst a coughing episode. Or prompt me by saying *'what was that BP again Willie?'* he'll suddenly mutter under his breath, just as I'm about to let a patient who was on the floor sit up, all without turning round beforehand. How does he do that? Watching me without me knowing he's watching me. Anyway he's certainly helped me and now my confidence is growing. I feel as ready as I can be for my first assessment at the end of my three months with him.

I think I've met most of Casildon-On-The-Hill's regular callers now. *'Guaranteed these ones will call right at the end of shift Willie'* Mac tells me. And it's true; we've had three late finishes in a row courtesy of:

Hattie Bower; an eighty eight year old lady. She's very sweet, but prone to falls. Normally its first thing in the morning when she gets up to make a cup of tea and her legs aren't quite with it yet. It doesn't help that she insists on wearing a pair of worn out slippers that her late husband bought her 20 years ago and she refuses to buy a new pair. *'You seen the soles of her slippers Willie? They're smoother than McDamnock's chin after a shave.'* Fortunately she hasn't fallen down the stairs so far, but that's because she has sanitary towels stuck on the edges of the stairs for extra grip. Every time we go there Mac says *'Hoicks her up Willie & away she'll go, just like a Duracell bunny.'*

Then there's George & Edna Buckett, an elderly couple in their eighties. He's been told if he has one more heart attack that'll be it as he's had six already. He has a history of falls due to wobbly knees caused by osteoarthritis. We normally go out to George after he gets up early in the morning; loses his balance in the walk in shower and does an unexpected dance as he falls to the floor. Every time we go there Edna will say *'he did it again last night!'* She then tells us the story that happens nearly every evening. He gets up out of his armchair and goes over to kiss Edna good night, she's sat reclined back in her chair, but as he leans forward puckering up for a kiss; he loses his balance and lands across her lap. She thinks *'Christ this time he's croaked it,'* but then she feels for a pulse in his neck to make sure George's ticker's still going, before a quiet voice can be heard from her lap saying *'Can ya get me up again please luv.'* After a lot of wiggling between the pair of them, plus using the electric riser to elevate them both up out of the chair, he's finally back on his feet again. Then he'll realise afterwards he's got his care-line wrist band on and could of called for help instead.

But, it's not just George on the floor that Mac and me have been out to them for. Edna always puts George's slippers under the grill to warm them up in the mornings. But one particular morning she forgot they were under there. So we ended up following the fire brigade out to them for a house fire. Fortunately they live in a quiet road that backs out onto fields on the outskirts of Casildon, so the fire engines were able to get down there and when we walked in; the whole house was smoked out, luckily no fire but there was a strong rubbery smell in the air. The material stuck to the grill tray looked much cremated, but still resembled the shape of a pair of slipper.

'You sure you didn't ask for smoked kippers George' Mac said to him. At least George saw the funny side to it.

Mary Chadwell's another 999 Casildon regular resident. A sixty four year old alcoholic psychiatric patient who I first met; well heard while at an AA meeting in the village hall. Apparently the only reason she bothers attending the meetings is to keep the social off of her back so she can still buy alcohol with her benefits money. And now I've been out to her at her home address too. No ambulance person is allowed to attend on their own, whether it be a solo on the response car or single-manned on an ambulance; now she's started exposing herself to crews at the front door and acting in an inappropriate manner if she gets a male crew attend. She's got big eyes that stare at you from all angles and her hair looks like it's had several thousand volts through it. Normally when we go out to her she claims to feel suicidal and wants us to take her to A&E to see the psych doctors. She's never self-harmed, but it is annoying how despatch will tell us it's safe to enter, all because she has told the 999 call handler she doesn't have any weapons on her. Yet when you walk in there's two samurai swords above the fireplace.

One different visit to Mary was at four o'clock in the morning because she had dyed her hair the night before. She wakes up at three in the morning with an itchy scalp, panicking and believing she's having a life threatening allergic reaction she dials 999. When Mac takes a look he tells her *'don't think this requires an emergency Ambulance lassie, you're having a reaction to your hair dye and apart from nits I can't see anything else wrong with you.'*

Nights always bring out the strangest of incidents, like last weekend on our fourth twelve hour night shift in a row, that point when you're feeling weary from having no social life at the weekend. We get a call to an unidentified male lying in a commercial waste bin; down an alleyway between two shops in the High Street. The call's come from the Police; two officers have seen a body dumped in the commercial waste bin with limbs hanging out query deceased. We aren't far from the location so I put my foot down to get us there, but just before we arrive despatch call us up to cancel us. *'The Police have now been brave enough to approach and found it to be a mannequin.'* Mac replies *'I'm good, but not that good lassie; can't revive a piece of plastic.'* As we've reached the high street when we get cancelled Mac says *'Willie slow down and put the side spot-light on so we can have a wee look down there.'* And as the side light from 0642 shines down the dimly lit alley; we see the figures of two officers fumbling around with the doll. We give a quick blast of the tartan trumpet and a wave before driving off; big smiles across our faces.

Another bizarre incident we attended was another visit to Casildon's nursing home 'Silver Hares.' *'A better class of living'* it states as its slogan. *This time* for a seventy three year old male. *'Apparently he's hanging upside down from a balcony on the first floor'* dispatch tells us. We arrive just before Police and fire-brigade turn up and sure enough, there is a resident male hanging upside down from the balcony with only his feet stuck in-between the metal railings stopping him from falling. He's alert and able to tell us he thinks he just leaned too far over. The fire brigade free him, but they have to keep him flat when pulling him back into the balcony because no one knows how long he's been hanging there. If he's sat or stood up too soon any build up of trapped toxins in the blood could lead him going into cardiac arrest. So he's laid on our scoop on the trolley and we take him to A&E for a check over. His obs were all within the normal parameters and he was chatting and laughing away with us about it. Unlike the manager of the nursing home, he wasn't too pleased when he received a phone call from the Police requesting he come in for a chat with them; as the senior nurse who should have been on duty on that floor was not in the building and no one else was left in charge on that level.

Needless to say the Police spent some time taking statements from all the staff and initiating a full investigation of the business.

No one knew how long the elderly patient had been hanging there; upside down with his feet stuck in the railings, just as-well the janitor smoked or it could have been a different outcome. It was quite a shock for the janitor when he went outside in the gardens, light up his cigarette and looked up.

It's very strange the things some people do. One night we get called to a community hall car park for a female with abdo pain. When we arrive there's only one car parked in the unlit grounds of the community hall. Mac goes up to the driver's door and knocks on it, then knocks again. After several attempts of knocking on the door to get the patient to open it, Mac opens the door himself. *'Did you call for an ambulance lassie?'* he asks in a rather loud voice. Without replying the patient just closes the door. This game of open and close the door goes on for about a minute, before the patient leaves the door open for Mac to talk to her. It turns out she had felt unwell and lethargic when she got in her car after work and stopped in that car park on the way home. She eventually explained that she didn't have the energy to carry on her journey so called 999. But it took a while to find all this out and she was very reluctant to talk to us. *'I want to see a Doctor'* she kept saying. But as to why she didn't want to leave the car door open and kept closing it on Mac; we could only guess was because she expected a Doctor to turn up not us in green.

It's not just patients who do the strangest of things, but family members also. While on scene with a ninety year old female who we attended to for a fall, we see through the living room window the daughter arriving in her car. As she pulls up outside; she drives straight into the car in front bumping it forward about two foot. She gets out and casually walks past without even looking to see if there was any damage. Once inside she didn't even speak to us that much, only a few words spoken when answering questions to Mac. We found out why from one of our other crew's Brett and Corrine. They've been out to the elderly lady many times and tell us that the daughter is the registered carer, but is fed up of having to go round there while at work when her mum falls over. She can't wait to get rid of the crew and get back to work.

You quickly learn in this job that not all accidents are accidental without human error playing a small or sometimes larger part. Take Stan Ford, Casildon's largest farmer in stature and build. Mac and me went out to his farm when he took his brand spanking new farming vehicle; an IH *Farmall high clear tractor* out for a spin in the fields. But as he drove between the birch trees and their overhanging branches; something which he had done on many occasions in his smaller tractor, he didn't realise how much higher the roll bar behind the seat of his new open cockpit was. As Stan Drove between the trees with his headphones on listening to his iPod, the branches quickly become entangled around the roll bar and were pulled down on top of Stan; trapping him in the cockpit.

When we arrive the fire brigade are there with three units on scene. Willoby the Wobbler is there too, sat with Stan who's now out of his tractor and sitting on a bench. Fortunately Stan's son had seen what happened and rushed over to help. Somehow though most probably due to feeling full of Adrenaline fuelled fear; he managed to pull enough of the branches out of the way so his Dad could get out. Apart from several minor cuts and scratches up both arms, the only damage was to Stan's pride over his new tractor still sat there covered in branches hanging over it.

'You're a lucky man Stan' Mac tells him. *'There's no way that tractor of yours was gonna fit under that tree.'*

I've heard about incidents involving unusual sex toys being used and then getting stuck, but fortunately I haven't come across any such incidents yet. Apparently one of the most common implements is the toilet brush; it gets inserted where only waste is meant to exit and whilst filled with pleasure the user gets a little carried away; causing it to get stuck (apparently). The excuse is: '*It was an accident, I fell on it.*' They seem to think we can just pull it out just like that, but '*We're clinicians not magicians*' as Mac would say. '*You're gonna need some more lubrication on that laddie, plus some muscle relaxant and that sonny is something we don't carry. It'll have to be done by the Doc in A&E.*' The look on their face when they realise they'll have to be seen by even more people while in that predicament is priceless.

Sometimes these accidents are caused by, well: '*Stupidity maybe a harsh a word to use laddie, but definitely a lack of knowledge...Knowledge is power Willie, can't beat a wee bit of knowledge*' Mac will occasionally remind me. Especially in the case of Rosie Front the fifty two year old female; who every Sunday would clean the nicotine stains off her finger tips with bleach and a nail brush. Only this particular Sunday while sat in her bathroom she'd run out of her usual cleaning bleach and used whatever else was lying around instead. She mixed them together thinking neither was as strong as her usual bleach, but the substance quickly began to bubble and let off an overpowering smell that nearly caused Rosie to pass out. After a very short time trying to get rid of the burning sensation from her face while she constantly coughs, she calls 999. When we arrive at the front door we're greeted by Rosie Front; water streaming from her eyes, her face looking very flushed as she stands there coughing non-stop. A strong chemical smell wafts past her and outside where we stand; 'Lassie *please tell me that ain't your perfume you got on there*' Mac asks as he begins to cough.

The smell's filled the whole house so we end up sitting in the back of the ambulance with Rosie, because it's too strong. Even Mac and me began to look like we're getting emotional with tears streaming down our faces. While I'm checking Rosie over, Mac looks at the labels on the back of the bottles. '*Rosie you mixed bleach with ammonia that combination causes chlorine gas to be released*' he says still coughing. '*It may have worked a treat on your fingers, but you also made what was used as chemical warfare during two world wars.'*

I've had my share of moments too, nearly bitten by a dog, vomited on a few times by patients; though now I see the early signs in a patient's face and get out the way quicker. And I've looked a twally too; slipping on wet grass while carrying the grab bag and ending up on my arse sliding down a muddy embankment towards a row of houses. But I suppose my most embarrassing moment would be when we went to a patient complaining of difficulty in breathing. We were advised to enter via the back when we arrive. And in my haste to get in I didn't realise the patio door wasn't open and smacked my face up against the glass before falling backwards onto the floor. Mac just stood there looking down at me and shaking his head. *'Willie, you're on your bahooky again, come on!'* as he steps over me and walks in. The patient who was having an asthma attack saw my disagreement with the glass door and began laughing, which then made her breathing problem even worse. Mac ended up giving her an injection of Adrenaline, because we couldn't get her breathing under control with a nebuliser.

But I'm not the only member of staff to occasionally get things wrong. There was Mac's previous crewmate Tim, his sister's married to a very well known British rock singer who's been around a few years. The station had a good laugh at Tim when he popped up on the front page of the Sun newspaper; snapped dancing with the famous singer's wife at a party, the caption read *'whose stole the rock stars wife then?'*

One night while he worked with Mac, he forgot to stow away the tail lift before driving off to the hospital. He thought it was a bit strange when the Police standing at the kebab and burger bar were waving frantically at him, but he thought they were just being friendly so he waved back. Then at A&E when he walked around to the back and saw the tail lift still lowered and realised why the Police were trying to gain his attention. Mac stands at the back door noticing his tail lift error; his eyebrows expressing his thoughts as he frowns. *'Timmy, don't tell me it came down on its own laddie.'* Tim loved the job, but couldn't refuse an offer to work for his dad, so a couple of months later he left to go work in the city on a much better salary.

I met him last weekend when he came to the station on Saturday evening, he was looking all dressed up and ready for a party. Brett and Corrine were asking how he was getting on with his much better paid job and how's things going with the famous brother-in-law. Timmy tells all about the brother-in-law rock star and his new job then interrupts himself by asking *'where is everyone for Bob's birthday get-together?'* Brett shakes his head; *'No Timmy that was a week ago.'* Tim was never known for having a good memory.

But, right now it's the start of another set of nightshifts. Willoby the Wobbler is flapping about something or other; think it's to do with leaving his portfolio paperwork on the response car's roof as he was about to get in and drive to another station, but as he's about to open the car door he gets a job and forgets the paperwork's still on the roof. Apparently it looked a spectacular sight, paperwork flying away in the haze of blue flashing lights as Dickey drove down the road. *'Dickie look on the bright side will you'* Mac chuckles as he tells him. *'At least you didn't lose any patient's details, only your own hard work.*

I myself am sat in the mess room with another McDamnock special brew and Mac's opposite with his head now buried in his newspaper; since Dickie's walked off in a huff over his paperwork joke. I've got a routine now with the special brew; I tend to sit on the recliner by the rubber plant, sip a tiny bit and when Mac's not looking tip some of it onto the base of the plant. Well I Don't wanna upset the old man and his love for his tea, but since I've been watering the plant it's developed quite a furry coat and grown somewhat, but no one's seemed to of noticed.

Anyway its twenty five minutes past the start of our shift and 0642's still not back yet, but they are probably on their way as I wonder what this shift and the next month will have in store for us.

Chapter 3.

The O/D Jay incident.

'It was going well till er..'

'For goodness sake' Mac cries out, as they read the next job coming through on the terrafix screen. '28 year old male unconscious, overdose on Heroin, police on scene. 'I can't understand why anyone would wanna do that, there's nowt wrong with a wee drop of scotch to give you a fix Willie' a frustrated Mac tells him.

'On looking at the address Mac recognises it as a regular caller. 'This'll be your first visit to O/D Jay then.'

'Odee? That's an odd name' Billy asks.

'No laddie O/D as in overdose, his names Jay; he's a bit of a numpty, but not usually violent to crews, just off his trolley. But don't forget; we never go in without the twallys telling us it's as safe as a house, or that the police are on scene. Can't get any sympathy from our lot if you get a skelpit.'

Some McDamnock words Billy can get his head around, or just nod and pretend he understands while trying to work them out later, but this wasn't one of them. 'What's a skelpit then?' he asks.

'Oh sorry, it's a slap. The twallys will just say; was your own fault for going in without waiting for the police.'

Arriving at the block of flats in Casildon's council estate they see a response car on scene, parked next to the Police car. Neither able to park in the area marked for emergency vehicles as the locals have parked there. Parking up in-front of the occupied emergency bay, Mac gives Billy some words of advice:

'Make sure you've got gloves Willie, you'll be wiping your feet on the way out of this one.'

They walk upstairs to the top floor; the noise of rowing couples can be heard in many of the flats. As they enter the patient's apartment; Billy notices the front door has several punch marks in the wood; the entrance hall is very dim no light bulbs work. The walls are undecorated and a stale, smoky smell in the air greets them. Walking into the lounge; there on the floor is the patient flat on his back in near respiratory arrest. Two police officers stand there with a member of the public; while Para Phil Smith kneels by the patient's head assisting his breathing using a resuscitation bag and mask with oxygen attached. Phil's kneeling down without touching the floor with his knees; a technique newbie's still have to learn as you don't wanna attach anything to your trousers. And on Jay's floor apart from cigarette ash he's no idea what's down there; it's clear that the carpet's not been hoovered for some time.

He gives a hand over to Mac as he continues to assist the patient's breathing.

'He took Heroin about 30 mins ago, his so called friend who gave it to him then did a runner when Jay went spark-out on the floor. He called this young man that's here with us now and told him to go round there as *'O/D's not looking good.'* 'When I arrived his 'Resp rate was knocking off, now down to four breaths a min and there's evidence of used needles lying around, so mind where you stand.'

Billy worryingly looks around and lifts his feet, checking underneath in case he's already trod on something.

'I was about to give him some Narcan' Phil adds. 'But haven't had time yet.'

'Willie, break out the Narcan will ya' Mac asks.

Billie gets a Narcan ampoule out of Phil's drugs bag. This'll be his first glass vial that he gets to break open, but worried he'll break the little glass bottle, he tries a little too gently to crack it open. Training school shows you the technique in opening them without breaking the glass, but without any actual glass vials for the students to practice on.

'Come on Willie put a little more effort into it' Mac tells him. 'But be gentle with her don't want it shattering between your fingers.'

Billy makes a small adjustment with the ampoule between his finger and thumb and gives it a little more effort...And then even more effort. Then on the third attempt...Success, a crack is heard as it breaks open in the right place without ending up shattered between his fingers. Once drawn up in a syringe Mac gives the dose slowly. 'A wee drop at a time Willie, or he'll be up like Zebedee demanding his money back for ruining his trip.'

Slowly O/D Jay starts to come round gagging on the plastic OPA tube in his mouth protecting his tongue from occluding his airway.

'Do you think we should give him some more?' Billy asks.

'No laddie, anymore and he'll be in your face' Mac replies.

No sooner had he said that then O/D Jay sits bolt upright; his gag reflex doing its job as it makes the OPA tube shoot right out of his mouth and fly across the room; hitting the wall opposite. They all watch the impressive projectile shot, then look back at O/D Jay who's now sitting there looking around and looking more confused than Billy trying to understand some of Mac's vocabulary.

'Easy laddie, welcome back' Mac says to O/D Jay as he's getting up off the floor and staggering about.

'Erm...what happened man?' He asks.

'You've been off your head me lad, on a wee trip' Mac tells him.

O/D Jay's friend then fills him in about his so called mate who had fled the scene and left him on the floor.

'Oh yeh, I remember now. He was here and erm...Yeh it was good.'

'You could have died mate with what you took' Phil tells him. 'You really need to cut this out Jay, if it wasn't for your friend here you may not have come back at all' Phil continues to add.

'I know…I know, but erm…yeh it was a good experience and erm…going well till…erm…erm…oh yeh.' O/D Jay stops in his tracks; now realising he had nearly stopped breathing and could have ended up dying this time.

Knowing what Phil said will just go in one ear and out the other; a pissed off Mac interrupts and gives him one of his well known Scottish phrases. 'Yer bum's oot the windae Jay. Ye went afore ye heid, if ye cannae stop this stuff, ye be a along time died.'

'Yeh man erm…yeh, I agree with what he said' O/D Jay replies; looking confused and none the wiser. Then looking at his friend; Jay completely forgets about his near death experience: 'Isn't that my jacket?' He says pulling at the material.

'You gave it to me two weeks ago Jay, don't you remember?' he answers back.

'Yer but erm…it looks better on me' Jay tells him. The two then start bickering about the jacket and forget about O/D Jay's near death experience.

'Jay we need to take you to A&E mate' Phil says butting in on their conversation.

'Nah mate I'm good; I don't need to go there. I appreciate like what you've done, but I'll be ok. Look at me I'm fine.'

Phil and Mac look at each other thinking the same thing: *Hardly fine, looks as rough as f…k, but then that's how he always looks cos he doesn't take care of himself.*

Several minutes go by with Phil & Mac trying to persuade him to go to A&E. *'In case you have a relapse and end up flat on your back again'* they repeat over and over to Jay.

Eventually they give up as a fully awake Jay looks back to normal; standing there rolling a cigarette, he ignores their advice and looks more bothered about persuading his friend to give him his jacket back. Billy asks Jay if he'll let him do another BP, but Jay's not listening anymore. So Phil finishes off his paperwork, emphasising that their patient has refused to travel to A&E and gives him a copy.

'Well Jay...We'll leave you two to get on with it then' Phil tells him.

'Yeh man thanks for coming...Much appreciated' O/D Jay replies in a strange, but grateful sort of way, then gets straight back to the discussion with his friend about who the jacket looks better on.

The three Ambulance men pick Phil's equipment up and with the police make their way out of Jay's flat. Walking down the stairs they can still hear Jay's discussion with his friend about the jacket.

Back down stairs an annoyed Phil puts the equipment back in the boot of his car: 'That's twice in a week now I've been out to him.'

'I know what you mean' one of the Police officers replies. We're often getting called to him as well, regularly asleep on a bench in the park or down an alley; he's one of the regulars now.'

'One of Casildon's regulars for you to remember Willie' Mac says as they say bye to Phil and the officers and get in the ambulance. 'You know laddie, one day we'll be going out to him and it'll be too late to breakout the Narcan. And as my mum would have said...*He ain't gonna live long and keep well, whatever will happen to him will happen and probably sooner.*'

Chapter 3

Sisters,

there's always a stubborn one.

Lillian is ninety two years old, she lives alone and was on her way to bed when she fell over in her lounge; tripping over those loose slippers of hers. She's hurt her left hand and has been unable to get up without the use of both hands. So she shuffled along on her bottom to the other side of the room and rang her sister who lives round the corner, asking her to come round and pick her up.

Gladys is eighty nine years old, she puts her cardigan and shoes on over her pyjamas and comes round to Lil's. Using her spare back door key to get in she tries to help her sister get up off the floor. Gladys holds under Lil's left arm, while Lil tries to push down on her right. They try to lift her, but struggle and no matter which way they wiggle, she ain't coming up.

'Come on Gladys, put your back into it' her sister tells her.

'I am Lil you're just too heavy Gladys replies back.'

After several minutes Gladys has to sit down on the sofa next to her.

'Lil it's no good I'm gonna have to call for the Paramedics.'

'No you're not calling an Ambulance I don't wanna go to hospital!' Lil snaps back at her.

'Lil I'm gonna end up on the floor with you if we carry on' Gladys stresses to her.

'Gladys...No, I'm not having an Ambulance, you know they cart you off and before you know it you're stuck in hospital for weeks.'

'It's no use Lil...You're gonna have to have the Paramedics.'

'You promise they won't take me away Gladys?' Lil worryingly asks.

'Yes Lil of course I promise' Gladys says nervously, her fingers crossed behind her back.

Halfway through a night shift and Casildon's Ambulance station has a strong fishy smell of salmon in the air as Mac has just cooked and eaten his dinner. They've just finished their meal break and Mac's now sat down with a McDamnock special brew and is flicking through the pages of yesterday's newspaper. Billy's sat next to the rubber plant with his mug of McDamnock brew; sending a late night text to Samantha. *Trust me you don't wanna be here with the smell of Mac's dinner still lingering around. Nite nite sexy Xxx.* Message sent he reclines back in his chair; just as the radio goes off.

'Come on Willie this is no time to be getting comfortable on your bahooky.'

'What we got then?' Mac asks as they make their way down the dark lane in 0642, out of the Ambulance station and onto the High Street.

'It's a fall, female of ninety two still on the floor.'

'This should be right up your street then laddie,' Mac says smacking his lips with the taste of his salmon dinner still lingering in his mouth.

Arriving at the address the front door is open. Knocking on it as they go in Mac says; 'Peek-a-boo ambulance crew.' Gladys comes out into the hallway to meet them.

'This way' she says. 'It's my sister Lil she's on the floor in here.'

They find Lil still sat up against the sofa.

94

'Hello Lil how have you ended up on the floor?' Billy asks as he kneels down next to her.

'Well young man, I was getting ready to go up to bed' she tells Billy. 'And then I fell onto the floor. So I bummed my way over here to the phone and called Gladys.'

Billy pauses *'unusual way of putting it'* he thinks to himself.

'Didn't you remember you've got your care line pendant on?' Mac asks.

'Oh yes I forgot that was there, silly me' Lil answers with a chuckle.

They check Lil's blood pressure, pulse and legs are ok, before getting her up off the floor.

'Your left wrist looks slightly deformed and swollen Lil' Billy tells her. 'Can you still move it as normal?'

'Well it hurts when I do, but as long as I keep it still; doesn't hurt at all...It'll be ok by the morning.'

Looking at the swollen wrist Billy says 'I think you may have a little fracture there, I think we should pop you up to A&E.'

'Oh it'll be ok, what can the hospital do?' Lil politely replies.

'Well they would give you an appropriate support to put around it; to help it heal and some pain relief to come home with' Billy encouragingly tells her.

'But it doesn't hurt if I don't use it' she insists.

'But Lil, you'll need to use that hand again won't you' Billy says; trying to persuade Lil against her stubbornness, knowing that she'll struggle on her own without getting that wrist looked at.

'Its fine young man, it'll be better in the morning' she stubbornly replies.

'But by the morning lassie' Mac interrupts; trying to help his crewmate out. 'It'll probably be a wee bit more swollen and painful. And even if you could get an appointment with your GP, he'll still want you to have X-ray lass...Tell you what Lillian, let's see if you can get up.'

 Lil tries to get up, but can only manage to lift her bottom off the sofa a little bit without needing to use both hands. She puts her left hand down onto the sofa to help lift herself up, but when she puts any pressure on her wrist she has to sit back down quickly because of the pain. 'You'll have to help me up young man' a bossy Lil tells him.

'But how will you manage when we've gone? Billy asks.

Lil doesn't answer; she just gives him a look of disgust.

Billy looks at Gladys and asks 'Do you live with Lil?'

'No I live around the corner, but I can't stay with her' she replies.

'So Lil you'll be at risk on your own won't you' Billy says to her.

Lil looks away from Billy. 'No...No...I ain't going; they end up keeping you in...Gladys this is your fault, you promised they wouldn't take me away.'

'But Lil you can't use your hand' Gladys tells her sister. 'You need to listen to the Ambulance driver.

'Lil doesn't answer her sister, she just looks away and now starting to get upset, a tear slowly runs down her face.

Trying another tactical approach; to persuade Lil that she needs to get that wrist looked at for her own safety Billy says; 'Lil what if it was Gladys who's hand was fractured and she lived on her own...Wouldn't you want her to go to hospital?'

A long pause follows before Lil answers him, because she knows what she should say...But instead she says 'not if she didn't want to, no...I wouldn't expect her to go' an immovable Lil answers back.

Seeing his crewmate has come to a brick wall, Mac joins in the debate again. Kneeling down next to her he says 'Lillian listen sweetie, all we would like to do is take you to A&E to get your wrist looked at. That doesn't mean you'll end up in hospital, we're only talking about A&E...I don't think they'll keep you in for a wee fracture to your wrist lassie.'

'How will I get there then?' she asks.

'We'll take you there...In the ambulance of course' Mac replies.

'Will you come with me Gladys?' Lil says pleading with her sister.

'But I'm in my pyjamas Lil, I'd have to go home and get changed.'

'You live round the corner Gladys don't you?' Billy asks.

Gladys nods.

'So Lil, what about if we stop at Gladys's on the way so she can get changed.' Billy looks at Mac to make sure that's ok with him.

'Aye of course' Mac says along with a nod.

'Ok then' Lil answers. 'As long as Gladys comes with me.'

'Yes Lil, I'll come with you' Gladys tells her sister with a sigh of relief.

'Well I need to go to the toilet first' Lil says to Billy.

'Ok do you want a hand up?' Billy asks.

'Yes please young man.'

After helping Lillian up, he walks with her to the toilet in the hall way next to the front door.

'No not that one, I use the one up stairs' she says as she leaves Billy standing by the downstairs toilet and makes her own way over to the stair-lift and sits down on it.

'I don't use that one at night I'm superstitious,' she says as she goes slowly up stairs on the chair.

'Do you need a hand up there?' he asks as Lil reaches the top.

'No thankyou young man, I'm quite capable with the one I've got.

While they wait for Lil, Mac and Billy admire the paintings on the wall. 'They were done by Lil's late husband' Gladys says.

One of the paintings they're looking at; is a beautifully detailed scenic picture of a small harbour.

'That's Looe in Cornwall' Gladys tells them. 'You see that girl walking along the pavement by the water...That's me, looking a bit wonky though aren't I' she says feeling a bit disgruntled with the artistry in the painting.

Several minutes pass while the two men look at the paintings again and again. Occasionally calling up to Lil to make sure she's ok, before returning to view the gallery again.

'Yes I'm fine thank you' she shouts down to them.

Eventually Lil comes back down on the chair lift.

'Gladys you're gonna have to sort my skirt out I can't get it on properly' Lil says to her sister, her skirt half tucked in around her waist; after having decided to attempt getting changed while up there.

The two men wait in the living room, while Gladys goes into the hallway and sorts Lil's skirt out.

'That's better' she says once Gladys has sorted her wardrobe malfunction out. 'But my wrist's hurting now,' she says to Billy as she rubs it.

'That's because you've been using your arm' Billy tells her. 'Do you want me to put it in a sling to give it some support.'

'No don't be silly, I'm ok' a steadfast Lillian tells Billy.

Several minutes then go by with Lil pottering about before she's ready. 'I need to take another shirt with me' she says to Gladys; who sees one lying on the sofa and puts it in Lil's bag for her. Then after Gladys walks off to do something else, Lil then comes along pulls that one out and puts in another one she's found. The same happens with Lil's cardigan, Gladys puts one in the bag and walks off, then Lil comes along pulls that one out and puts another one in.

'I'm starting to doubt we'll get to the hospital before the end of shift at this rate Willie,' a bemused Mac says.

Then just as they're both about to sit down while being as patient as they can be; after managing to persuade Lil to attend A&E. Gladys suddenly says 'Right I'll go out the back door, lock it and meet you round the front then.'

'Is it not easier to lock it from the inside' Billy asks Gladys. 'Then you can come with us out the front, rather than walk round a dark alley' he suggests.

'No I have to go out the door I came in young man, I'm superstitious too' she tells him.

'You can't win with these two Willie, they're a spritely pair' Mac tells his crewmate.

Refusing a carry chair to take her out to the ambulance and preferring to hold onto Billy's arm, Lil finally walks out to 0642 while Mac locks the front door.

'Just pull me in' Lil demands to Billy at the steps to the side door.

'You sure you don't want me to put the tail lift down and use that to go up on?' Billy asks.

'No...no just hoicks me in,' the ninety two year old insists.

Billy gently helps her up the two rather steep steps into the Ambulance, then as he settles her down on the trolley Lil says 'I wish my son Roy was here, he fusses over me.'

'That's good of him' Billy replies feeling a little worthless after all the hard work and patience he and Mac have put in; in order to do what's best for her.

Gladys meets them at the ambulance, climbs up the steps unaided and sits down as Billy's putting the blood pressure cuff back on Lil's arm.

Mac is still knelt down at the front door, struggling to get the key back out of the keyhole. After a couple of minutes, the sound of Mac's voice can be heard as he mutters to himself, 'can't get the *dafty key out of the bloody door now.'*

Hearing this from the back of the Ambulance, Gladys says to Billy 'Tell him he needs to turn it sideways first, then pull it out.'

'Mac you need to turn it sideways, then pull the key out' Billy shouts out to him.

'Ok young man' Gladys says 'I think the whole street heard.'

'Sorry Gladys' Billy says to her now feeling like a little school boy told off by the headmistress.

Following the instructions the key comes out with ease. 'Finally' Mac says. 'Boy this job's a test to your patience laddie' he tells Billy as he walks over to the Ambulance.

Getting in Mac starts the engine and finally off they go; around the corner to Gladys house.

Now the ride in the back of an ambulance is always a bit bumpy, especially with the air suspension that these vehicles are fitted with, they tend to bounce around no matter how smoothly you drive. This causes some people to comment on how rough the ride is and makes the driver feel as if they were to blame. 'A *box on wheels, that's all it is*' Mac would say. But eighty nine year old Gladys doesn't hold off and comment's on the ride as soon as the vehicle's off.

'What's this got, square wheels?' she tells Billy who can only smile at the very witty comment.

'Willie let the twallys know we're making another stop before getting to the hospital, just in case they think we're having a laugh and hanging this job out.'

Billy calls up despatch and explains the reason for the delay on scene and the reason why they're making an extra stop.

Stopping round the corner, Gladys gets out and makes her way to her front door. While they wait for Gladys, Lil asks

'Do the Doctors work at night?'

'Yes Lil, the Doctors work nights too.'

'Do woman nurses work at night?' she then asks.

'Yes Lil, woman nurses work at night too.'

Ten minutes pass as they wait for her to return.

'Willie I hope Gladys ain't got short term memory loss,' Mac shouts through into the back.

'Why's that Mac?'

'Cos she may have forgotten why we've dropped her off and gone to-bed instead.'

Eventually a fully dressed Gladys returns, sits down and with seat belt on and what seems to have been an eternity of a job; 0642 finally make its way to Casildon General.

Chapter 3

'That wasn't there a minute ago'

'Red call for you 0642' despatch tells Mac and Billy. 'Female 31 years old, 38 weeks pregnant, contractions every 2 minutes and her waters have broken, car en route.'

'With these lassies Willie, we either load and go if they're mobile enough or stay and deliver if they can't move...The back of an ambulance isn't the place to give birth...No room in there for two patients' Mac tells his crewmate as they leave Casildon General. 'A lassie's first bairn will take longer to come, but once they've dropped the first; anymore will come on out with just a wee cough' he continues to add. Billy nods with a vague understanding of Mac's strange explanations.

Its 03:30 in the morning; three quarters of the way through a Monday night shift, fourth and last out of a run of nights. 'How you feeling Willie...Are you used to these nights yet?'

'Getting there I think...I'm not quite like a zombie now; compared to a few weeks ago.'

'Aye, it takes a bit of time to adjust; it's a bit of a beastie being up all night.'

Arriving at the address; they're met by Para: Sue Berry, the patient and the patient's husband; all walking out of the house together towards the ambulance. Sue's laughter greets them before they even get out of the vehicle. In her strong Norfolk accent resembling the actress Olivia Colman she introduces the patient in her cheerful voice 'This is Amena she's 38 weeks pregnant, waters broke twenty minutes ago and her contractions are less than two minutes apart...She feels rather restless and is unable to keep still; bless-her, hence why we've come out to you.'

103

'Petal try to get yourself comfortable on the trolley' Sue says to an anxious Amena who looks worried about sitting down on the trolley. She looks around at her husband and starts talking to him in a distressed voice in her native language. 'This young handsome man is Ahmed' Sue says as Amena grabs hold of his hand. 'Amena only speaks a little English, but Ahmed can translate for her. Though Billy you might have to translate for Mac.'

'There be no problem understanding Mac' he tells them; unimpressed with Sue's joke.

'Ahmed me lovely; try and get Amena to settle down on here for us' Sue asks. He tries to calm her down and eventually gets Amena to sit down, but not without getting straight back up a couple of times first before finally she leans back and puts her legs up on the trolley. But still restless she moves from side to side as she holds out her hand for her husband.

Sue continues with her handover 'I've spoken to Maternity, so they're aware Amena is on her way and Ahmed's got her maternity notes. I have offered Entonox, but Amena bless-her declined. I did manage to get one blood pressure reading...Eventually, though Amena was a little reluctant to keep the cuff on. It's all written down for you on the form me cocker. Right, I'll leave yous to it then. All the best Amena, Ahmed' she says as she opens the back door. Looking back at Mac she winks 'Good luck Macky' she says to him before getting out of 0642 whispering 'you're gonna need it.'

'Right then Amena, let's try to get another blood pressure from you' Mac says as Billy puts the blood pressure cuff on her arm. As it inflates Amena stares at Billy, then down at the cuff as it continues to inflate, then straight back at Billy again.

'Amena try and keep still just while the cuff tightens, I know it's not very comfortable' Billy says to her trying to calm her down. 'Why don't you have another go with the Entonox again' he asks, offering it to her.

Mac asks Ahmed to explain to her that it will help with the contractions. She takes it from Billy's hand, takes one deep breath on the mouth piece and throws it back at him; just missing Billy's face. Then the BP alarm goes off indicating it's timed out after the third attempt to get a blood pressure, Amena's restlessness causing the monitor to fail at getting a reading. Billy decides to have a go with a manual BP instead. He puts the cuff around her arm and the stethoscope ear-tips in his ears, but when he places the chest piece under the cuff on her arm Amena begins to stare at him again. As Billy inflates the cuff Amena's eyes widen and suddenly she pulls her arm away; taking the cuff and stethoscope still with Billy's ears attached with her. The ear-tips yank from Billy's head. 'Ouch' he says softly, managing to reframe from saying anything stronger. 'Ok...maybe I won't try that then.'

Mac asks Ahmed 'Can you ask if Amena feels the urge to push?'

The reply is vague, but 'No' seems to be what she is telling Ahmed.

'Ok Willie let's get goin, don't think we should be hanging around any longer' he says to Billy.

As Billy drives through the dark lanes to Casildon General he can hear the sound of Amena restlessly turning on the trolley from one side to the other and Mac's voice constantly saying 'Lassie try to calm yourself down and try some Entonox? It will do you good.' Again she takes the mouthpiece from him, takes a deep breath on it and again throws it, this time at her husband. After the third time of asking and the third time of the mouthpiece being thrown at her husband, Mac gives up before she ends up hitting him in the face with it. The blood pressure cuff's the next thing to go airborne. As Mac presses the button, the cuff inflates and when it begins to get tight Amena pulls it off and throws it at Mac; hitting him across the face. For a moment the big man just sits there without flinching; a quick look to his right to compose himself, he picks it up and puts it away.

Arriving at Casildon General and turning left off the main roundabout into the hospital grounds. Amena stops turning from side to side. Her eyes open even wider and with a look of concern on her face she looks at Mac, then down between her legs lifting her jogging bottom trousers up, then looks back at Mac.

He thinks *surely you've not had the bairn without a wee bit of notice lassie.'* Amena now with a worried look on her face points between her legs. Mac gets up holding on to one of the hand rails as he peers over and looks in the direction that Amena is pointing. Those McDamnock eyebrows rise up as he sees a baby laying there on the trolley sheet between her legs. The baby is motionless with no sign of breathing; it lies in a pool of amniotic fluid.

'Willie you need to stop now! I need you in the back' he shouts through to the cab. Mac lifts the baby up still attached to the umbilical cord, the baby's purple coloured face is floppy in Mac's arms, he rubs his cheeks to stimulate him to breathe. It only takes a couple of circular rubbing motions before the baby starts crying aloud. 'There you go wee man' Mac says.

Billy unaware of why Mac needed him to stop immediately, especially as they're entering the hospital opens the back door and is surprised to see Mac with a baby in his arms. 'Willie we'll need the maternity pack out so we can use the towels from it' he tells Billy as he gets in.

With one towel placed on Amena's belly, they use the other to dry him off and place baby on mum's lap; giving baby a minute to rest. Then Mac passes the cord clamps to Billy 'Willie cut the cord for us please laddie.'

Feeling a little nervous about cutting his first cord Billy picks up the clamps and remembering what they were taught in training school puts the first one in place. Then as he's about to put the other clamp over the cord, Mac readjusts Billy's hand position. 'There you go...A wee bit more of a gap than that needed laddie. Not too close to the bairn's bits.' Billy clamps it down and picks up the cord scissors. 'Don't forget a firm grip is what you'll need and make sure you've got the scissors in the right place Willie' Mac says teasing and testing his crewmate's nerves.

Billy places the scissors around the cord and grips the handles. Keeping his composure he squeezes the handles together, then together some more. *'God, this is tough'* he thinks to himself as the blades are not cutting through it.

'Willie will you give it some welly' Mac whispers as he peers over Billy.

Squeezing even harder the scissors finally cut through, *'that's more like cutting through gristle'* a relieved Billy thinks to himself.

They wrap the baby up in the clean towel. 'Gotta keep the wee bairn warm laddie, that's very important. Then Mac has a quick listen to the baby's lung sounds. The baby's loud crying can be heard through his steph as he tries to listen. 'Well there's no doubt he's chest is clear' Mac says lifting his steph off his ears and rubbing one of them. Billy puts a paedi sats probe on one of the little boy's big toe's while Mac jots down his obs on a new form, now they have two patients.

'How you doing Lassie' Mac asks.

Amena looks at Mac with a smile: 'We're good thankyou' she replies before looking back down at her newborn.

Right then Willie, we've gotta: Pulse of 160, Resps of 36, chest is loud and clear, oxygen levels of 100%. The wee bairn's face is now a good pink colour; all limbs present, five digits on each and baby's now crying well. Time of birth: 04:07. Place of birth: Outside Casildon General maternity unit. Shall we continue the rest of the journey then?'

'Yes Mac' Billy replies looking at his mentor; whose not had one bead of sweat run down that forehead of his towards those eyebrows. He's been cool and calm all the way through.

A thirty second drive later and they are parked outside the maternity department. Taking a much calmer, now smiling Amena and new addition in on the trolley, they are greeted by Marion the midwife who looks surprised to be greeted with an extra patient.

'I hope you're not trying to take on all our work Mac' she says.

'This wee fella didn't want to wait any longer, must of heard Marion was on shift' Mac jokingly replies, before explaining what had actually happened. Into one of the rooms they go with Amena and onto the maternity trolley, just in time as Amena's eyes widen again and now restless once more she grabs hold of Billy's coat; pulling him towards her as the contractions start again for the placenta to be expelled.

'We'll have none of that grabbing in here!' Marion tells her, placing Amena's hand firmly back down onto the bed and shoving an Entonox mouthpiece in her mouth. 'Now breathe this in and keep your arms on the bed dear!'

Billy straightens his coat as Mac says goodbye to Amena and her husband.

'Never argue with a midwife Willie' Mac tells him. 'These lassies don't take shite from anyone.'

'That's right boys, now be gone with ya' Marion commands them. 'But I'll let you have a cup of tea from the staff room on your way out...Just to show you're good looking young crewmate I'm a nice person really.'

'That's the kind a bossing about Mac likes...Marion you're all heart' he says to her as they leave the room. Then when he thinks they're out of sight Mac whispers 'some say, Marion can send any woman into labour with a wee touch of her hands and make them deliver just by shouting at them.'

'I heard that Mac' she shouts at them.

'Aye Marion, just teaching the wee laddie here...Just teaching him' he replies as they walk down the corridor.

Chapter 3

Fait Accompli.

'Hey Willie have ya still gotta sting in your bahooky?' Mac asks taking the Mickey out of him after he fell over while trying to jump a railing on their previous job.

'Yes, yes very good Mac' he replies.

The memory of Billy leaping over the railing is still the talk of 0642 or at least as far as Mac is concerned, as they return to station. It's still putting a smile on Mac's face; the vision of Billy leaping over the railing, holding onto it with one hand while he swung his legs over. Three quarters of the jump was looking good; just shame about the landing, he came straight down on his backside on the other side.

Its five pm on a clear sunny afternoon as they make their way back to station, now within their last hour of the shift they're hoping to finish on time for once. It's been another long day starting off with an elderly gentleman with a UTI; believing there was a hostage situation going on next door. Before leaving with the patient Mac did confirm with the neighbour's that they didn't have their hands tied behind their backs and weren't being held at gun point for ransom over gambling debts. Then there was an RTC, but they got cancelled within a minute of getting the job as it turned out to be a bystander calling 999 for a squirrel he'd just witnessed get run over. That was followed by the usual array of: an abdo pain, a maternity though just the usual *'materna-taxi'* run; nothing stressful. An elderly lady fallen in the bathroom and landing in the bath, a 36 week pregnant lady with chest and abdo pain after eating too many pancakes and a collapse in a car on the M6: *'It's a classic American car, red in colour on the hard shoulder with male collapsed underneath'* the details read; given by a third party caller who's witnessed it from the other carriageway despatch inform them. When Mac & Billy turn up the driver of the car walks over to them & tells them about the problems with the gearbox and then looking at them confused asks 'So what are yous doing here?'

'Were you lying underneath at any point?' Mac asks.

'Yeh to look at the gearbox' the man replies.

'Aye, that figures' Mac says bewildered.

So after leaving the M6 and continuing their journey; Mac comes out with another quip about Billy's incident with the railings, but realises it's getting a little tiring now so changes the subject to Billy's growing confidence. 'You're beginning to shine me laddie, you'll make a grand Para.'

'Thanks Mac, of course I owe it all to my mentor; he's taught me a lot, some of which has even been useful too.'

Mac looks at Billy with a frown on his face after realising Billy's witty reply. Just then the terrafix alarm sounds as another job comes through on the screen. 'Better text your lassie Willie, let her know your be late for dinner again.' A familiar sentence Billy has gotten used to over the past two and a half months. Pushing mobile to scene on the Terrafix; Billy reads the job details: RTC, location on the Motorway, M6 southbound between junction 39 and 38. A lorry and two cars involved, three patients, entrapment.

Then the radio goes off as despatch calls them with further details. 'We're getting several calls on this one 0642, believed to be after junction 39, Two children involved, believed to be trapped at time of call, Helimed is refuelling and will be en route soon with a doctor on board. Fire and Police also on their way, ops manager will be attending and there's a rapid response car running, but I think you are the closest at the moment. Can you give us an early update from scene? Over.'

'Roger' Billy nervously replies. Mac's usually cheerful or sarcastic response to a job is replaced by silence. 'Do you think it could be serious Mac?' Billy asks.

'Can't be sure Willie, but it is the busiest time of day and that stretch is a wee bit high up over the hills, but I've never known it to be an accident black spot area.'

Billy hasn't attended any serious or fatal RTC's yet, the patient's have always been up and out of their vehicles prior to his arrival, or sat there in their car complaining of neck pain. He's not even dealt with an entrapment yet. Thinking about the incident they're on their way to his palms begin to sweat as he puts his gloves on in anticipation. 0642 rejoins the motorway at junction 39 southbound and the traffic's flowing smoothly across the three carriageways. Mac drives in the outside lane with the blue lights flashing and intermittently using the sirens to remind the drivers in front to look in their mirrors. Billy looks out at the unsuspecting drivers who are not aware of the delays they are to come across shortly.

'There's over twenty miles between these two junctions, that's some distance to go if it ain't up this end' Mac says.

Ahead on the slow winding and downward carriageway they can see brake lights, as the traffic is slowing down. Eventually Mac has to move over onto the hard shoulder to continue now the traffic's coming to a standstill. Keeping the sirens on constantly and slowing down, Mac drives cautiously in case some impatient driver decides to pull over onto the hard shoulder in front of them. Billy looks at Mac who's still looking relaxed and composed; 'I *wonder how many serious RTCs he's been to in the past?*' he thinks to himself as he begins to feel really, really nervous. Although he knows if this RTC's bad Mac will take over, he can't help feel there's a lot of pressure's on him. He also starts to wonder how he will feel, as he's never seen anything before like the horror he will undoubtedly face one day in this job. Even the beautiful scenery around them is not distracting Billy's concentration on the motorway's horizon, which is now full of stationary traffic that seems to go on forever.

Finally, around the next slow and winding bend the motorway reveals an end to the sea of standing cars; beyond that the motorway is empty. At the front of the traffic queue is a distant and blurry view of abnormally positioned vehicles. Too far out of sight to be seen clearly, the view still stands out as an unusual one for a motorway. Now getting anxious, Billy's eyes fix to the view in the distance at the end of stationary traffic. Slowly the abnormal view begins to get clearer as the blurry objects start to take shape. The shape of a blue van sat alone on the inside lane can be made out, beyond that an articulated lorry is jack-knifed with its trailer across the first and second lanes of the carriageway with what looks like a grey car crushed at the front of it. But there's no blue flashing lights from any other emergency service vehicle on scene yet.

'So we're first on scene then Mac?' a nervous Billy says.

'Can't believe we got here before the water fairies,' Mac replies in a quiet tone; not hint of sarcasm in his voice.

Getting closer to the scene it becomes evident that the grey object against the front of the lorry is a car; it's crushed up to the windscreen against the cab of the HGV.

'Jesus I hope there's no one in it' Billy's uneasy voice says.

'I wish I could agree with you, but there's too many people gathered near-by for my liking' Mac's replies, his voice sounding apprehensive.

Reaching the end of queuing traffic and unable to proceed much further due to the carnage spawned across the road, Mac turns the sirens off. An eerie quietness surrounds them until they get close to the crowd, then they hear the screams coming from people calling them over. Pulling over near the group of people they grab their high Vis jackets as they depart the vehicle. Billy gets the grab bag, while Mac goes straight over to the car that the crowd of people are standing near-by. One witness joins Mac as he walks over.

'I saw the van cut across from the outside lane in front of the lorry, it broke hard, but then jack-knifed and the cab...oh my God' he pauses, before saying 'it erm...the cab it went into this car on the inside lane crushing the driver's side onto the hard shoulder. The van driver and lorry driver are over there, but erm...I haven't seen anyone get out of the car...When I called 999 the call handler said *'don't get anyone out of the car in case their injured, wait for the Ambulance to arrive.'*

'Thankyou young man' Mac tells him as he pats him on the back, leaving him standing there he carries on towards the car.

'Excuse me may we have a little room please everybody!' Mac shouts to the crowd as he approaches the car. The driver's side is crushed by the cab of the HGV and blocking any access to the driver's door so Mac makes his way round to the passenger side.

As Billy runs over he thinks *'shit how can anyone still be alive in there.'*

'There's a little girl in the nearside rear seat laddie, can you deal with her' Mac shouts over the roof of the car to him.

The rear offside door is dented from the impact to the front of the vehicle; unable to open it Billy goes around to the other side. He takes the grab bag off his shoulder and drops it to the floor between him and Mac. Pulling on the nearside door handle; it's stiff, but Billy's able to open it enough to lean in, there sat on the nearside seat he sees a young girl still strapped in; crying. Breathing fast she sits there ridged, her fingers clench together; she stares straight ahead whispering 'Help me, somebody help me.'

'Hey...I'm Billy what's your name sweetie?' Billy asks in a soft voice as he kneels down and offers his hand out to her.

'Rosie' she replies, her voice broken from crying.

'Rosie, that's a beautiful name...How old are you Rosie?' Billy asks.

'Ten...I'm ten' she quietly replies.

'Have you got any pain anywhere Rosie?'

'My neck feels stiff and my back hurts' she tells him.

'Ok Rosie, I need you to keep your head really still for me while I feel down the back of your neck, don't nod or shake your head, is that ok?'

'Yes' she replies.

'Wow, you're a brave girl Rosie' Billy tells her as he places one hand on her forehead while he gentle palpates down the back of her neck with his other hand.

'Ouch that hurts' she says, as Billy's hand gently presses down to the bottom of her neck.

'Does that pain go any lower?' Billy asks.

'Yes, it goes down my back...I'm scared' she says as tears run down her face.

'Rosie you're doing so well, but we need to keep your head really, really still, so I'm gonna hold my hands either side of that beautiful face of yours and help you keep still, ok?'

'Ok' she answers.

'There we go' Billy says as he moves her blonde hair to one-side and places his hands either side of her face knowing that's the position he and Rosie will have to stay in till more emergency crews arrive.

Rosie's eyes turn towards Billy and in a distressed voice she asks: 'How's my Dad and brother? They won't answer me, I've been shouting at them to say something, but they won't answer.'

Billy turns to look at Mac attending to the young boy in front of them. The boy is sat motionless, while Mac leans over feeling for a carotid pulse in his neck. Mac looks at Billy and shakes his head as he starts chest compressions. A cold shiver runs down Billy's entire body as he begins to sweat. Scared to look back at the little girl, he knows he has to look into her eyes and tell her something, something to keep her calm in the confined space they're in. *'She's waiting for an answer'* Billy thinks to himself. So taking a deep breath in and summoning up all his emotional strength he looks into Rosie's eyes, a confused expression forms upon her face as she stares at him unable to stop sobbing. He can see her eyes looking all over his face, waiting for him to tell her why they've not said anything back to her.

114

'Rosie' Billy says. 'My colleague's helping your brother right now, but he's very poorly at the moment and that's why he hasn't been able to answer you.'

'But what about my Dad, he's not said anything either?'

Again Billy looks at the front of the car; Rosie's Dad is slumped towards the middle, the driver's door and dashboard are crushed up against him. Billy begins to get angry with himself as he realises that training school hasn't prepared him for this, what to say or how to deal with this kind of horrific situation. *How do I tell her that her Dad and brother sitting in the front seats are most likely already dead?*

Looking into her deep blue eyes Billy feels a rush of adrenaline run through his body as he fights his emotions; trying to find the right words to say. 'Rosie when more of my colleagues turn up they'll look after your Dad. But right now I want you to focus on me. Keep your eyes on me don't look at anything else, don't worry about anything else. We're gonna concentrate on making you better ok, can you do that for me?'

'Ok I'll try' she replies quietly.

'That's it Rosie, you're doing very well.'

As Billy's mind focuses on Rosie, he doesn't hear the sound of more sirens getting louder as two traffic Police cars arrive on scene. Two officers get out of one car and take charge of the scene, while the officer from the other car goes over to Billy. 'Is there anything I can do for you?' he asks.

'Can you support Rosie's head for me while I get some equipment' he asks standing up; still holding her head still. Suddenly Rosie's trembling voice says 'Where are you going? Please don't leave me, I'm scared.'

Billy looks at the officer; he's desperate to get on with some obs, but kneeling back down again he looks back at his patient. 'Ok Rosie I won't go anywhere, I'll stay right here until my colleagues turn up.' Realising he can't go and help Mac or do any checks on Rosie while she's feeling so scared; he makes himself comfortable next to her again.

'Thank you' she replies; still sobbing as she clutches Billy's arm for a moment before resting it back down again. At that moment station manager Dickie who's been sent to manage the scene arrives. Getting out he heads straight over to Billy. 'Mac's probably gonna need you in the front' Billy shouts as Dickie makes his way over.

'Ok fella' he replies and quickly goes past Billy to the front passenger door.

There Dickie finds Mac performing CPR on the boy. He's trying hard to keep his heart going while still in a sat position as he's legs and waist are trapped by the dashboard's intrusion into the front. In a quiet tone so as not to alarm Rosie Mac speaks to Dickie while continuing chest compressions. 'We've got one adult patient deceased in driver's seat and two paediatrics. This boy approx fourteen years old had a very faint pulse on my arrival and minimal breathing effort. No pulse or resps now, but the little girl Billy's with seems to be ok at the moment.'

'Right I'll get onto despatch and update them' Dickie replies and turns around to walk off as he lifts his radio of his belt clip.

'The twallys can wait Dickie' Mac says hastily. 'I need you to maintain this boys head and bag for me.'

'Right...erm...yer of course Mac' Dickie replies as he clips his radio back on his belt and forgets about managing the scene for the time being.

As Dickie assists Mac with CPR, three fire engines arrive on scene and the air ambulance can be heard overhead, looking for a clear area to land. The fire units get their gear out and bring it over to the car readying it to cut the roof off, as they do; Phil on another response car arrives.

He runs over to Billy. 'What can I do for you?' he asks as he puts his hand on Billy's back to give him some reassurance more hands are here now.

'I still need to do a BP, but Mac's now got the grab bag' he replies feeling glad someone else has finally arrived to help him.

'Ok buddy I'll get it,' but as he goes around Billy to the front of the car; Dickie asks him to take over from him so he can manage the scene. 'Ok Dickie, but Billy needs help too, he's on his own back there' Phil insists.

Mac pipes up 'Dickie, he's been left on his own since we got here...Check on him will you.'

'Yes Mac will do' Dickie replies.

Trying to catch up with managing the incident he goes over to Billy while confirming with despatch where Helimed will land and requesting an ETA for another crew.

'Helimed will land on the carriageway up ahead of your position' despatch reply. 'And ETA for second ambulance crew is polling two minutes away...Over.'

'Billy, are you ok there fella?' Dickie asks.

'Rosie and me are ok aren't we?' Billy answers back while still looking at Rosie's face, smiling to try and reassure her he's not leaving.

'What do you need then?' Dickie then asks.

'Someone to do a BP for me and see if fire can get the offside door open please' he asks Dickie while still looking at Rosie.

'Right I'll get onto that for you' Dickie says as he disappears again.

A minute later a grinding noise begins on the offside rear passenger door as the firebrigade get to work on opening it just as another ambulance arrives. Donna and Bob, who've been working out of another station on this fateful day, are the next crew to arrive and park next to 0642. They see Billy and the little girl on their own and head straight for them.

'Do you want me to take over?' Donna asks Billy as she kneels down beside him.

'No…I'm ok thanks, Rosie's being a very brave girl for me and she wants me to stay with her, but I've not been able to get a BP yet…Dickie was supposed to get the cuff out of Mac's bag, but I guess he's got sidetracked again. Phil's with Mac though.'

Looking up over the rear door, Donna quietly replies. 'I know…I see them.'

While Donna stays with Billy and Rosie, Bob grabs the manual BP cuff for them before going over to 0642 to get a neck collar. Donna's just about to squeeze in with Billy and get a BP from Rosie when at last the rear door that the firebrigade have been working on gives and is bent open. 'Billy' Donna says. 'Once I've got a BP why don't you stretch your legs for a while, I'll carry on holding Rosie's head.'

'Don't think this little girl's gonna like that, she's gotten used to me.' 'Rosie' Billy says looking back at her. 'This is Donna she's gonna stay and help us. She's gonna keep your head still now, is that ok?'

'No…No I want you to' she cries; grabbing hold of his arms so he can't move.

'Tell you what, what if I go around to the other side now it's open and I can sit next to you and hold your head, how about that?'

'Promise you're not leaving me' she says to Billy, her voice sounding nervous.

'I promise, I'm getting straight back in and staying with you, ok.' Rosie smiles back at him. 'Good girl Rosie.' Then, swapping over hand positions with Donna on Rosie's head Billy gets out and goes around to the other door.

'Has he been looking after you?' Donna asks Rosie.

'Uh-huh' she replies, without moving her head.

'He's good like that…And not bad looking either; is he' she whispers to Rosie who manages a small giggle at Donna.

'You girls just go ahead and talk about me as though I'm not here' Billy says as he gets back in the other side, sits down next to Rosie and then takes over holding Rosie's head again. 'There that's more comfortable' he tells her.

Back from 0642 Bob passes Donna a collar. 'Mac wants my help so I'll be at the front.'

'What's that? Rosie anxiously asks.

'It's just a little something to help keep your head still, but first I need to check your blood pressure, is that ok?' Donna asks her.

'As long as it doesn't hurt' she answers back looking even more worried now.

'It'll squeeze your arm a little, but if it squeezes too much, you just squeeze Billy's arm, ok.'

Rosie manages another small giggle. 'Did you see that Billy' Donna says. 'That's twice Rosie's laughed now.'

'And at my expense too' Billy replies. Finding Billy's reply a slight distraction; Rosie giggles again.

'Wow, that's a beautiful giggle you've got there' Donna says as she gets her stethoscope out of her pocket. Placing it in her ears, Rosie's eyes concentrate hard on what Donna's doing as she gently places the cuff around Rosie's arm, puts the head under the cuff and slowly inflates it.

'Ouch...Ouch...Ouch,' Rosie murmurs.

'Squeeze my arm Rosie with your other arm' Billy tells her. She raises her hand up to Billy's and holds onto his arm. 'That's it; squeeze it harder than that cuff's squeezing you.' Squeezing his arm as much as she can; the sound of a small giggle and cry at the same time comes from her mouth. 'Wow, that's some strong grip you've got there Rosie' Billy says which makes her giggle and cry even more; taking her mind of the blood pressure cuff around her arm.

119

'Got it, well done Rosie' Donna says as she releases the cuff and takes her stethoscope out of her ears.

'Ok, now we need to put this collar around your neck to keep your head really, really still' Donna says as she picks it up.

'I don't like it, that's gonna hurt even more.'

'Let's just give it a try Rosie and see if it does...And if it does hurt more then we'll put it round Billy's neck shall we.' A small giggle escapes Rosie's mouth as she's not sure whether to find that funny or not. Bringing the collar up to Rosie's neck Donna brushes Rosie's blond hair out of the way. Rosie begins to get even more anxious and as it's put around her neck, she starts to cry. 'No...It hurts, I don't like it' she cries out.

'It's ok...Rosie, it's ok' Donna says brushing a tear away from her cheek. 'We'll leave it off for the moment, as long as you keep really still for us, while Billy holds your head. Can you do that?' Donna asks.

'I will,' Rosie replies.

'Shall I put it round Billy then?' Donna whispers to her.

'No he'll look silly' she answers back with a smile.

'He will won't he' Donna replies, then looks at Billy. 'Well, it looks like we're not going anywhere for a while, so putting it on can wait.'

Round the other side Bob takes over chest compressions on the boy, while Mac goes over to Dickie who's liaising with the Police and Fire officers; advising them on how he wants to manage the patients.

'Wobbler we need to get this boy out now' he tells Dickie interrupting their conversation.

'I'm on it Mac' Dickie replies, as he continues discussing the course of action on how to get the two patients out. Mac starts to get impatient, with his hands on his hips, he starts biting his lip to prevent himself from opening his mouth and voicing his own opinions on how to get them out.

'Ok fella' Dickie says to the fire officer before turning round to Mac. 'Right, I've told fire the roof's gotta come off to get the girl out, but the priority is getting the boy out…So they're gonna work around our guys cutting the front door off before cutting away at the front nearside wing and dashboard to free him…I've asked them to place a canvas between the front and back to protect the girl from seeing what's happening.' Dickie continues explaining his plan while Mac stands there still biting his lip to stop himself interrupting. 'Once they've freed the boy and you've got him out, the roof can come off to get her out. Helimed will take the boy; the doctors are on their way over now with a stretcher and Lucas chest compressor. Then, you and Billy can take the girl in 0642.'

'Aye Dickie sounds like a plan, never doubted you for a minute' Mac replies patting his former crewmate on the back before going over to 0642 to get his and Billy's hard hats.

'How long's it gonna be before we can get my brother and Dad out?' Rosie asks.

Donna and Billy look at each other as they try to think of the best thing to tell her.

'Sweetie' Donna answers a very worried Rosie. 'We'll have everyone out as soon as we can, I'm sorry it's taking so long.'

Meanwhile, Dickie doing what he does best and managing the scene; comes over to them, takes Donna to one-side and explains how they plan on getting Rosie and her brother out.

Leaning back into the car Donna explains to Rosie what's going to happen. 'We're going to get your brother out first, but the firemen need to place a sheet between us in the back and the front while they cut away the door.'

'Why do they need to cut the door?' Rosie asks fearfully.

Wiping a tear away from Rosie's face Donna says 'because it's a little difficult to get him out, there's not much room in the front. My colleagues are going to be with him so don't worry.'

'As long as Billy stays with me' Rosie insists.

'Hey, of course I'm staying' Billy tells her.

Donna then gives a nod to the firemen to start. They tie one end of the canvas sheet to the B pillar between the front and back door on Billy's side, then slide it past him and across the middle of the car to the other side and secure it.

'Willie here's your hard hat, put it on!' Mac tells him as he passes by putting his own on and making his way round to the other side of the car; where Phil and Bob have been joined by Helimed's Doctors whose are now leading the resuscitation.

'How long's he been without a pulse now?' one of the Doctor's asks Mac'

'Must be over ten mins Doc...No sign of improvement since output ceased thou.'

'Well' the Doctor replies. 'He needs to be out of the car ASAP.'

With Rosie and Billy's view to the front now blocked by the canvas as the Doctors and Paramedics in the front work on the boy, the firemen get to work. The shattering of the front windscreen to remove it frightens Rosie.

'Shh...It's ok' Billy tells her, leaning his head closer to hers. She begins to shake as the noise from the cutting equipment starts tearing apart the hinges from the door. The sound of metal slowly being twisted and cut drowns out all other noises around them; as the hydraulic cutter tears through the front wing. Slowly the firemen cut their way through to the dashboard that's trapped the boy in his seat.

'I'm scared' Rosie cries.

'It's ok Rosie' Billy tells her. 'It's ok the noise will be all over in a minute.'

As each sound of cutting metal ends with a sudden snap and vibration, felt in the back by Rosie and Billy; so another one begins. Now getting very distressed and frightened Rosie sobs.

'How much longer will it go on for?'

'Not much more, it'll soon be all done. Close your eyes Rosie and keep them closed real tight that will help,' Billy tries to tell her over the noise, but now getting worried himself that this brave girl might not be able to take much more.

As he holds her head gently but firmly, he can feel Rosie's body beginning to tremble. Her hands grab Billy's arms tightly and although Rosie's eyes are squeezed shut; tears still run down her face.

'I can't take this... I can't...I can't' Rosie now cries, her head shaking against Billy's hands.

'You're doing really well Rosie' Billy tells her. 'You're such a brave girl...We're nearly there.'

'I can't, no I can't take it' she screams over the noise of the cutters.

Billy's now fighting to keep back a tear himself as he watches Rosie. Her face now full of tears looks frightened beyond belief as he tries hard to keep her calm and still.

But just as he thinks she won't be able to take this anymore, Mac's voice booms 'that's it we're clear!'

The sound of metal being torn stops, only the sound of the compressor can be heard. One of the Doctor's calls out loudly. 'On three...Ready, one, two, three' as they then lift the boy out quickly and place him on their stretcher and continue CPR.

'Rosie' Billy says firmly. 'Make sure you keep your eyes shut for me' worried that she may see her brother being taken away while the crew work on him. He watches Rosie to make sure she keeps her eyes shut, while out of the corner of his eye he can see the boy being taken quickly over to the air Ambulance.

Once her brother is out of sight the canvas is removed and laid across the front car seats to cover the occupant still trapped and inaccessible in the front. 'Hey, you can open them now' Billy says to Rosie.

Still scared, she slowly opens her eyes and looks around. 'Is my brother ok?' her voice quivers.

Not sure how to answer; Billy doesn't speak, he can't think of anything to say. But Donna leans back in the car again. 'He's gonna get a ride in our helicopter, but now, now it's time to get you out.'

More sounds of metal being twisted and cut fill the air again; as for the next few minutes the firemen cut through the pillars and lift the roof off. Sunlight now fills the space where Rosie and Billy are sat.

'Willie me lad you need a break, let me take over!' Mac tells him as he leans into the car after returning from transferring the boy to Helimed.

'I'm ok Mac' Billy tells him, but sounding emotionally exhausted.

'Please don't go anywhere' Rosie cries.

Being too emotionally wrapped up in looking after this frightened little girl; he's not had time to think about how he's coping, but reassures her anyway. 'Hey, don't worry I'm staying right here.' He then briefly looks at Mac, unable to engage in full conversation with his crewmate while focusing on holding Rosie's head; he tries to reassure him. 'Mac I'm alright, don't worry. I've been with Rosie all this time she wants me to stay with her at the moment.'

'Ok then laddie, if your sure' Mac reluctantly replies. He looks at his crewmate; concerned about whether he's coping with the emotional situation. Standing back up he looks at Donna. 'Keep an eye on the lad will you'

'Don't worry Mac, I am' she replies.

Leaning back into the car next to Billy she whispers to him 'I think he's just worried about you, he's not having a go.'

'But I'm alright' he tells her without even pausing to think about it.

'Ok' Donna answers back. 'But if you feel you need a break and wanna go stretch your legs even for a few minutes I'm right here, I'm sure Rosie won't mind.'

Billy nods. 'I know.'

Donna looks at Rosie. 'Sweetie what's gonna to happen next is we're going to put a board between you and the seat, then the firemen are going to slide you up onto it...It'll feel strange, but you'll be perfectly safe. It may bit a little uncomfortable, but we won't hurt you, ok...But first, remember that collar? We need to put it round your neck now.'

'Ok' she replies. 'As long as Billy's staying with me.'

'Rosie, I'll have to let go of your head when we start to move' Billy says to her. 'But Donna's gonna take over and stay right next to you, ok?'

Rosie starts to look worried again. 'Alright, but don't go Billy, don't go anywhere' she cries at him.

As they put the collar back around Rosie's neck, her worried look turns to fear again as it feels really uncomfortable. Her breathing begins to get faster and she starts crying. Trying to keep her calm, Billy softly speaks. 'You'll be ok Rosie, trust me.'

Mac returns with the spinal board, scoop and trolley, everybody takes up position around the back of the car with the board resting on the boot. On Mac's command the spinal board is placed between the seat and Rosie; who's looking more and more frightened as each moment passes. Then as Billy's at the head end he gives the commands to lift. Fighting his own emotions to cry, he looks at her tear streaked face, But manages to control himself as he says to her: 'You need to be really...really brave for me now, I've got to let go in a minute as we slide you out, but I'll be right here I promise.' He looks up at everyone around him. 'Are we ready?' making sure everyone's in position. 'On three then' Billy says out loud. 'One, two, three.' They slide her up the board one bit at a time, pausing as they go to readjust positions. The sound of Rosie crying is beginning to get louder as Donna standing at the side of the car takes over holding Rosie's head.

'Ok I'm on' she says to Billy, as her hands take over holding Rosie's head still. But before continuing with the lift she leans next to Rosie. 'Shh...It's ok sweetie your being such a brave girl, we're nearly there now.' She gives the command for the final lift as Rosie is then raised fully onto the board and out of the seat. The board is laid flat on the back of the car, resting on the opened rear and boot for a moment; before Donna commands everyone to slide Rosie and the board onto the trolley. Then they place a scoop under her and remove the spinal board out of the way; their patient is now ready to be strapped in before transferring to 0642.

Billy steps out of the remnants of the car, his fingers feel numb with the sensation of pins and needles running down to his fingertips. He opens and closes his hands several times trying to get the feeling back into his hands. Then taking off his hard hat and taking a deep breath in, he looks at the carnage around him: Ambulance equipment litters the nearside of what remains of a car's frame. Sections of torn metal that were tossed aside by the firemen lay spread either side of this shell. But, he's quickly distracted by a familiar voice. 'My Dad, what about my Dad' Rosie voice screams out. Now unable to see Billy's face she screams, repeating it over and over. Mac and Donna try to console her, but she doesn't listen to them. Billy rushes round and manages to get to Rosie's side as she's being strapped to the scoop. Now restless and agitated she's trying to push them all away. She fights against the crew who are all feeling emotional about the distress she's going through, as they try to help her. 'Rosie its Billy' he says firmly; holding her hand and looking down at her face. 'I'm here listen to me sweetie, you need to calm down for me' he says as he strokes her hair. Seeing Billy's face again her rapid breathing eases, her clenched fists relax and she lowers her arms again. 'That's it Rosie' Billy softly tells her. 'That's better.'

Once she's calmed down, Donna looks at Billy and smiles with recognition to his magic touch. Then leans closer to Rosie while holding her head still and in a soft voice says: 'See, he's not just a handsome boy is he?' Rosie smiles and a tiny stifled giggle escapes her mouth before she quietly continues to sob. 'Hey, no more tears Rosie, not now Billy's here.' Donna tells her. 'I know your being such a brave girl, but we need to place these blocks either side of your head now, just to help keep you still till the Doctor has seen you at the hospital, ok sweetie?'

'Ok' she whispers; squeezing Billy's fingers together.

Continuing to hold onto her hand, Billy looks into her eyes and smiles. 'It'll be ok.' Then when he's sure she's calm enough, he rests her hand back down on her lap, picks up the head blocks and gently places them either side of her head. Maintaining eye contact with her he brushes her hair away from her forehead; before placing the first of the two straps across the blocks. Once the second one's in place he wipes a tear away from her cheek. 'There, all done now Rosie. I know it's not very comfortable, but it won't be for long; it'll be taken off as soon as the Doctor's seen you.' She reaches for Billy's hand and squeezes his fingers again. Satisfied she's settled down Billy gently places her hand back onto her lap and steps out of the way so Donna and Mac can push the trolley with Rosie on towards 0642.

Now left standing there on his own; Billy feels a pounding headache coming on and the tiredness creeping up on him. Again he looks around at the carnage, for a moment just watching the Police starting to clear up the twisted metal lying across the carriageway and the firemen preparing their equipment around the other side of the car; as another patient is still to be removed once Rosie's been taken to hospital. An eerie silence fills the air now there's no screaming or shouting voices, no sound from the fire equipment, only the sound of 0642's engine and the fire engines nearby. Billy tries to take in what's happened over the last hour, but is unable to get his head around this traumatic event. *'Maybe it's because I'm too tired'* he thinks to himself. Just then his thoughts are interrupted again by that familiar voice. 'Billy, where are you?' Rosie cries out. 'Where are you?' she hysterically screams again. Turning around to the direction Rosie's voice, he sees Rosie's arms reaching up the air again; waving frantically about for the one person who's kept her calm. He runs over to her as they transfer her onto the tailift and holds her hand again. 'I'm here...I'm right next to you' he tells her as he squeezes her hand trying to comfort her. Mac takes Billy to one side.

'You've done well laddie, but you need a break. Bob will drive us to the hospital and Dickie will take you back to station. I'll meet ya back there for a brew' Mac tells him; concerned that he's got too emotionally involved.

'Mac, I think I should come. As long as she can see me she's calm.' As they discuss this, Rosie's voice continues to cries out for Billy as she is taken up on the tail lift and into the ambulance. Billy's looks at Mac desperate to go with. 'See...You need me in the back with her Mac.'

'Aye laddie that maybe the case, but I'm concerned about you coping with this, you look emotionally drained and paler than ever.'

'But I can't just walk away from this right now...You know you need your crewmate in there with you...Please Mac.'

Mac's eyebrows frown as he looks concerned about this situation. 'Hmm...Don't think this is a good idea, but we ain't got time to discuss it...Get your bahooky in there then.'

'0642 here, got a trauma call for you' Mac tells Casildon A&E on the alert number.
'Paediatric female, ten years old, second patient involved in RTC on M6. Rear

passenger, wearing seat belt. No loss of consciousness, complaining of C3 cervical tenderness, radiating lumbar area. No other obvious injuries, motor sensory circulation all four limbs ok.

Blood pressure: 114/78.

Pulse: 108.

Resp rate: 24.

BM: 5.1.

SP02: 100% on air.

GCS 15, ETA 20mins.'

As Bob drives 0642, Billy's sat at Rosie's side holding her hand and keeping her calm. Mac monitors her; does another BP and starts his paperwork. He leans over to Billy and whispers. 'The Police officer said they've taken Rosie's mum to the hospital. let Rosie know her mum's gonna be there when we arrive...but Willie, obviously her mum's gonna be very distraught with the bad news so be aware of this when we open the back doors.'

'Ok Mac, thank you' Billy replies. He tells Rosie she's gonna see her mum soon, then for the rest of the journey asks Rosie to talk to him about her favourite toys and TV programmes, to keep her mind off thinking where her brother and Dad are.

As 0642 arrives at A&E, a large gathering of people await they're arrival. Bob turns the lights off as he parks in the resus bay. The sounds of sobbing and screaming outside can be heard inside 0642 as they unplug they're equipment. Billy starts to feel anxious about what Mac said to him regarding the emotional environment about to be thrust upon them any moment now. Taking a deep breath in he prepares himself as best as he can as Bob goes round the back, opens the door and puts the tail lift down. Several people gather at the back doors and one woman rushes into the back screaming

Rosie's name and trying to hug her while she's strapped to the scoop. Rosie starts crying again on hearing her mother's voice.

'It's ok baby, mummy's here now' she repeats to Rosie.

Billy lets go of Rosie's hand and gets out of the way to give the two of them some room. Mac looks at Rosie's mum. 'Mum, Rosie's only laid flat for what we call mechanism of injury. There's no obvious damage from what we can see,' hoping this will give some reassurance to a mum who's just had her world shattered.

'Ok, thankyou' she replies crying.

They go straight into resus, Rosie's mum holds her hand tightly, both of them crying as the crew push the trolley with Rosie on. As they head for trauma bay number two, Billy notices the other trauma bay is empty and wonders where her brother has gone. Once they're in bay two, they line their trolley up next to the hospital one. The bay's full of doctors all waiting to start their assessment as Rosie is gently transferred on the scoop over to the A&E trolley.

Mac gives a handover in that powerful Scottish voice of his as all the Doctor's stand motionless, attentive to his every word. Billy's wants to say goodbye to Rosie, but with so many staff in there he's unable to get near her again. And with so much going on around her, Rosie doesn't even notice where Billy is as she focuses on looking at her mum standing beside her; holding her hand tightly. But before Billy leaves, he manages to squeeze in-between the staff and gently squeeze Rosie's other hand. Letting go of her hand he takes the trolley out of the cubicle leaving Rosie and her mum together with the doctors. He takes one last look at her looking up at her mum, then closes the curtain behind him. Taking a deep breath in, a feeling of relief and sadness fills him as he goes over to a wash basin in another cubicle and washes his hands. Seeing another nurse cleaning some equipment, he asks 'What's happened to the boy from the RTC?' She turns around looking at him upset.

'I'm so sorry, they ceased resuscitation just before you arrived, there was no improvement on the way in on the air ambulance. They think he had massive internal bleeding...He's been put in a quiet room now his sister and mum are here.' She wipes a tear away as she looks over to the trauma bay Rosie is in, before looking back at Billy.

'Oh my-God, that's terrible news for the mum,' Billy answers back. Words fail to describe how he feels as he walks slowly out of resus with the trolley. In fact, the next few minutes seem like a blank to Billy as he puts the trolley away and cleans up the back of 0642. He doesn't even remember Bob saying *Donna's followed them up in their ambulance to take Bob back and they'll meet them at Casildon station in a bit.*

'Ok, sure Bob see you in a bit' apparently is what Billy said, but he only remembers sitting down with his head in his hands. Several minutes then pass, with Billy sat alone.

'Willie, tea for you' Mac says, as he opens the back door. Billy lifts his head; wiping a tear from his face he takes the plastic cup from his hand.

'Thanks Mac' he says with a lump in his throat. He stares at the cup for a moment, before clearing his throat and taking a big sip from it.

'Dickie's just rung' Mac says as he sits down next to him. 'He understands it's been a long day and we're past our finish time, but he's requesting all of us involved have a debrief before we go home.'

'Sure' Billy replies without looking up and just staring at the cup in his hands.

'Billy...If you need time to yourself, I'll tell Wobbler the debrief will have to wait till tomorrow.'

'No that's ok, let's get it done tonight while still fresh in our minds.' He looks up at Mac. 'Do you know that's the first time in nearly three months you've called me Billy?'

'Aye Billy, about time I think' Mac replies. 'Remember laddie, I'm here for you if you need to talk.'

'Thanks Mac...I'm ok at the mo.'

'Well then let's get back; I'll drive while you finish your tea off.'

Looking out of the window on the way back, Billy feels empty. The evening light fades as he watches all the cars and people going about their normal lives. They're blissfully unaware of the terrible events he has witnessed and the horrific pain and sadness one particular family now face. Still unable to make sense of it all he wonders how this torn apart family will cope and come to terms with their loss. He looks over at Mac and thinks how does he and all the other staff deal with being part of an event like that. How can you be so closely involved and then; just suddenly walk away from it and carry on, either with the next job or go home at the end of a shift and have a normal evening and return the next day to do it all over again? Without having any answers to give himself and unable to get to grips with it all he feels uneasy as he closes his eyes.

'Billy come on, we're here' Mac says waking him up now they're back at the station.

'Sorry Mac for dozing off their' Billy replies, his voice sounding croaky as he wakes up.

'No worries,' Mac tells him as he gets out of the vehicle. 'Looks like we got company then,' looking at the car park now full with other emergency vehicles. As they walk inside, the station's full of voices, all talking loudly over one and another. 'Seems Dickie's offered for everyone to come back to ours and have a party; how cosy, just what you don't need right now.'

The room's full of conversations all about the RTC. Donna, Phil and Bob are sat on their usual recliner armchairs. The leading fire officer and a few firemen along with the three Police officers from the incident are gathered around the table and two high ranking Police officers have turned up too; waiting to take statements from all involved. Plus there's the night crew Brett and Corrine, who have been waiting to take over on 0642. At that moment Dickie walks in to the messroom. 'Right everyone I've asked you all here to discuss how you felt the incident was managed...Who wants to start off then?' Several voices pipe up at the same time.

'Fellas...Fellas, one at a time' Dickie exclaims as he stands up to interrupt them.

As the conversation continues, Billy's unable to concentrate on it his mind's elsewhere. He tries to listen and focus on the opinions given by the different services on what may have been done differently, but Billy who was involved right from the beginning doesn't join in. Whereas Mac doesn't have any problem vocalising his points of view, but as well as expressing his opinion; he's also keeping an eye on Billy at the same time. He notices his gaze keeps wandering off out of the window into the darkness.

'Too much F...... time taken Dickie, to decide how to get the boy out before actually doing it...You can't do effective CPR while sat upright in a car seat, you know that' Mac tells everyone deep in conversation over the delay. But when the fire officer and Dickie reply, Mac doesn't say anything in return as he's noticed Billy has got up and gone outside.

'Fait accompli Billy' Mac says as he sits down on one of the garden chairs and joins Billy outside in the yard where it's quiet. 'It means something that's over and done with. Done before we get there...Don't blame yourself lad, I shouldn't of let you stay so long with the little girl.'

'No Mac you tried to tell me, but I didn't listen...I thought I was handling it ok at the time.'

'Human nature Billy' Mac tells him. 'Whether it's in this job or not. When you get drawn into an emotional situation you can't see what's going on around you...You did well and held it together when it mattered laddie, many others would have lost it with emotion before we got to the hospital.'

'Mac I can't get the image out of my head, that little girl asking about her brother and Dad.'

'In time Billy, in time you'll learn to live with what's happened...Doing this job; you'll see things that your loved ones and friends may never witness in their lifetime. These things you'll get to see collect as little dust bunnies in the back of your mind, they'll never go away' Mac tells him.

'But maybe it's made me realise something...Maybe, this isn't something I want to witness again Mac' a confused Billy tells him.

'Go home and rest in the bosom of your loved one Samantha. Give it a few days, I'll tell Dickie you'll give the statement in a day or two, but you need some time off first.'

'Thanks Mac, but I don't think my minds gonna change' an adamant Billy tells him.

'We'll see Billy...We'll see' an optimistic Mac replies.

Billy shakes his head. 'I feel I've let you down Mac.'

'You've only let me down if you don't get your bahooky back here in a few days, now be gone with you' Mac tells him.

Billy takes a slow drive home, no radio on just silence as he drives. As he opens the front door a worried Samantha comes rushing up to him, throwing her arms around him she holds him tightly. She's been anxious all evening not knowing what was going on. With only a few brief texts earlier saying: '*Be late home luv as we're on way to an RTC.*' Followed by a quick update while at the Hospital telling her: '*Don't know yet when I'll be home babe, it was a nasty job.*' Samantha's used to him coming home late after a shift, but never this late and it's left her worried all evening. She offers to make him something to eat, but he doesn't feel hungry. So with a bottle of beer sat on the coffee table in front of him, Billy lays on Samantha's lap on the sofa. She gently strokes his hair while he explains the tragic events of the job he and Mac attended, but in the back of his mind thoughts of the last few months as a student Paramedic run through his head.

'I don't want to do this anymore Sam...I can't do a job where I have to carry these images and probably more around every day.'

'Shh...Go to sleep Billy, go to sleep' Samantha tells him; continuing to stroke his hair.

Slowly the images in Billy's mind fade as he drifts off to sleep.

Chapter 4

Nightmares

'Billy why isn't my brother and Dad talking to me? Billy, don't leave me!'

*Oh shit...*Another bad dream. It's three in the morning; I'm soaked in sweat as I sit up in bed. It's been two weeks since the fatal RTC, I've still not returned to work as the images of that day are still crystal clear in my head. Most nights I wake up from the same dream with sweat pouring from me and Rosie's voice still ringing in my ears

So after sitting on the edge of the bed for several minutes I get up and go into the bathroom to wash. As I look in the mirror over the basin I don't even recognise myself; I just see an empty shell. *'When will this feeling ever end?'* Is the question I keep asking myself? The only way I can see out of this is as I told Mac *'I need to move on and find something new, close the nightmare door behind me.'* Mac's not happy with that idea, *'can't close the door on something that'll stay with you forever. You need to give it more time...Time to learn how to accept what happened and live with the memory, only then you'll be able to move forward,'* that's how Mac sees it. He's been texting me every day, checking in to make sure I'm ok. I lie and reply *'yes I'm fine.'* But I'm sure he knows different. He's even offered for Samantha and me to go over theirs one night; join Maggie and him for dinner. He's even promised not to shove a McDamnock special brew in front of me, which would be just as well as they probably don't own any rubber plants for me to tip it into. Sam's nagging me to go, but I just don't feel like going out.

I've had texts from several of the guys at the station and both Donna and Kerry have rang offering to meet up and chat *'Well I'm here if you feel like talking'* they both keep telling me in their domineering ways. *'Don't be stubborn Billy don't try to bury it all.'* Maybe they'd manage to scare the nightmares out of me. Anyway, Best try and get some sleep I guess. As Occupational Health wants a chat in the morning. They are coming down to the station at ten and Mac has insisted he wants to be there with me. I tell him I'll be ok, but he said *'those occi health girlies will have you signed off with stress for 6 weeks and you'll end up in a daze, not good for your career.'* I'm glad he'll be there, if anyone can kick my arse into gear it's old Mac.

Chapter 4

Crossroads

It's nine thirty in the morning; Billy arrives at the station for a ten o'clock meeting with occupational health. Mac is already there chatting with Dickie in the manager's office.

'Hey Billy me boy it's good to see you' Mac says as he gets up.

'Hello fella how you doing?' Dickie asks Billy as he stands up to greet him too.

'I'm ok, feeling better than I was a week ago' Billy replies to them.

'I'll go make a cup of tea fellas,' Dickie offers. 'While you two catch up.'

'No need Dickie what Billy needs is a McDamnock special brew' Mac says as he tries to make his way out of the office first.

'Mac the boy needs a proper cuppa, not one of your bitter brew's' Dickie answers back as he's already beat Mac out of the office and heading towards the kitchen.

Left standing at the office door Mac frowns. 'Huh, he wouldn't know what a proper brew looked liked if it came up and bit him on the bahooky' he whispers to himself. Then turning to Billy he asks. 'Well how you been then? And don't give me any crap Billy.'

'You know bearing up,' Billy begins to tell him. 'Nights have been the worse, waking up with nightmares.'

'Aye Billy I've been there too' Mac tells him. 'It's a dark place to be. I feel for you.'

They go and sit down in the mess room where Mac talks about how it's been working with Kerry for the past few shifts. 'Oh she's a feisty one alright, sometimes I have to calm her down and keep her cool just so she doesn't get any complaints coming in against her.'

'Here fellas, a proper cuppa' Dickie says putting two mugs in front of them. For the next ten minutes they continue to catch up over Wobbler's cuppa; Mac's face showing a look of distaste with each sip of the tea; as he puts it down quicker than he picked it up. Then right on time the two ladies from Occupational Health arrive, Dickie greets them at the door and takes them into the mess room. 'Billy this is Judy and Pam. Ladies, this is Billy and this...This Is McDamnock TC, who'll be accompanying Billy,' Dickie says giving them a hint of Mac's fiery character in his introduction. 'Please use my office, I'll go make you two ladies a cup of tea before you begin.'

'Willoby Wobbler's grovelling' Mac whispers to Billy, as they make their way into the office. 'Aye, knew he was up to something, when I smelt his aftershave earlier.'

They sit down and Judy begins to explain why they have requested this meeting.

'Billy I understand you have been out on front line duties for about two months now.'

'Yes that's right' he answers.

'And I understand you attended a fatal RTC involving a young boy and his father where you dealt with the younger sister at the time who was traumatised in the incident.'

'Yes that's right' he replies.

'Lassies excuse me for interrupting' Mac says 'but we already know why we're here, so can we move on please.'

Pam looks at Mac 'And who are you Mr McDamnock.

'I'm representing the lad because, I've worked with him, since he came out on the road.'

Judy then asks Billy 'and you didn't want either of the two union reps, that are based here to attend with you today?'

'Erm...they both offered to, but both of them suggested Mac attends with me.'

'And why's that?' Pam asks.

Mac leans forward. 'Pammy, I was working with the lad on the day of the RTC...I have taken him under my wing to help him through his first three months and that includes any setbacks...So the reason I am here is to make sure the outcome of today is what Billy wants and what is best for the lad not what someone behind a desk thinks is right for him, because they've read about it in a book.'

Pam now leans forward meeting Mac halfway across the desk. 'Mr McDamnock...I've worked as an Occupational health physician for ten years, I think I'm qualified enough to decide what is best for someone who's experienced a very traumatic event.'

'Aye lassie' Mac replies as he relaxes back in his chair. 'I'm sure you are, but never the less you won't allow them to return to work gradually and at their own pace. You either sign them off with stress or they have to return to front line duties full time, with only a short period of third manning...How many of these poor souls have ended up leaving the service after returning to work and being made to feel like they are mentally unfit for frontline duties' Mac eagerly asks.

'Well I can't comment on that' Pam stutters. 'We do not keep statistics on those that leave the service.'

'Ahh yes, your statistics Pamela' Mac replies, as the meeting begins to feel like it's turned into a courtroom battle. 'Do you get out on the front line much Lassie? Or are ye too busy collecting your other types of precious statistics?'

Pamela pauses, before answering. 'Mr McDamnock, shall we return to matters at hand and not get side-tracked.'

'Fine by me' Mac answers back as he folds his hands together.

Moving on; Pamela focuses on asking Billy to describe the events that happened that day and how he has felt since. Billy doesn't go into too much detail about the incident, but explains how he has felt since and ends with 'the voice of Rosie wakes me up every night.'

'So Billy' Pam gently asks. 'Do you feel something different could have been done to prevent you from now feeling this way?' as she turns to look at Mac with a look on her face that may suggest he is to blame for Billy's situation.

Billy pauses and thinks about all of the events that day. 'No, Mac kept asking how I was coping, he asked one of the other crew on scene to keep an eye on me while he was dealing with a paediatric arrest and he insisted several times I take a break and let someone else take over with Rosie...But it was me who refused as she wanted me by her side and I was acting in the patient's best interest.'

'So being the senior clinician Mr McDamnock should have made sure you took a break, shouldn't he have?' Pam inquisitively asks Billy. Mac leans forward again, his eyebrows moving towards each other as he has a look of disgust on his face.

'Relax Mr McDamnock, relax' Pamela says. 'I know all about the incident I've read the report. I understand how the two of you were dealing with different patients at the same time and how stressful the situation was. I'm not here to put blame on you...Now Billy, what do you want to do?'

'I don't know' he replies, not knowing whether coming back is what he wants to do, but at the same time not wanting to let his crewmate down either. 'Since the RTC, it's made me think maybe this isn't for me and that I should have a change of direction in career.'

'And how serious have these thoughts been Billy?' Pamela asks.

Billy looks at Mac, then looks down at the table in front of him, with his hands clasped together.

'If I may interject' Mac says changing position in his chair again, moving from his usual relaxed back in a chair posture to sitting upright and resting his folded arms on the desk; he's keen to put his point across. 'In my experience anyone who has a bad experience within their first year ends up quitting. Cos too much time off leaves them doing too much thinking...Which in turn leads them to leave the service..And probably leave for the wrong reasons too.'

'So Mr McDamnock Judy asks. 'What do you think is best for Billy?'

'Well I think the lad should come back out on the road with me, a wee bit at a time to get back into the swing of things...If you feel up for it of course' he says looking across at Billy.

'This has to be Billy's decision Mr McDamnock' Judy insists.

'Judy, Mac's right' Billy says. 'I should give it another go and not be too hasty with any decision.'

'Billy are you sure that's what you want to do?' Judy asks. 'Without any persuasion from Mr McDamnock that is?'

'Yes...Yes it is' he replies. 'If I don't do it now I fear I'll be one of those unknown statistics which go under the radar that Mac mentioned.'

'Ok' Pamela tells him. 'But if you feel it's getting too much you must tell your manager or let us know and we'll review the situation.'

Mac interrupts again, 'so none of this two week phased return to work and then you're out full time malarkey...You'll let the lad do it at his pace then?'

'Yes' Pamela answers. 'We'll let him do it your way.'

Mac smiles and looks back at Billy. 'You ok with that laddie?'

'Yes Mac' he tells his crewmate.

'Well I think that's it for now' Judy says. 'I wish you all the best Billy.' She stands up and offers her hand out to shake Billy's.

142

'Thankyou' Billy replies as he stands and shakes Judy's hand. As Mac gets up and shakes hands with Pamela; their eyes meet in a strange confrontational stare. This tense gaze between the two seems to last a long time; neither wanting to show an ounce of defeatism. Eventually they part hands and the two ladies walk out of the office; stopping to have a quick chat with Dickie on their way out to the car park.

'Well Billy you sure you're up for it?' Mac asks as they walk out of Dickie's office.

'As much as I can be' he replies. 'Like you say Mac the longer I stay off, the more I'm gonna think about leaving.'

'That's me boy. Seems to me your at a crossroads, let's see if old Mac can steer you in the right direction.'

'I don't know if you can Mac I can't see it happening.' Billy says feeling sure his minds made up and nothing's going to change that.

Chapter 4

Billy's revivification

It's been three days since Billy's meeting with the two Occupational Health ladies and he's agreed to come back on a dayshift with Mac. Though he's not sure it will make a difference he's willing to try for Mac's sake.

Its 05:30 the sun's starting to rise on what looks like being another beautiful day, as Billy pulls into the station car park and notices 0642's on station. *'Unusual for the night crew to be back before the end of their shift, but good for them to get to finish on time for once, '*Billy thinks to himself as he gets out of his car. As he walks across the yard to the station Mac's green Jaguar roars into the car park so he stops and waits for Mac to join him. There's the usual loud bang from the rear of Mac's car, followed by smoke shooting out from the exhaust as Mac gets out waving his hand in front of his face to clear away the smoke.

'Gotta get that exhaust fixed one day' Mac says. 'But hey it's good to see you back.' He adds as he puts his arm around Billy's shoulder and they walk in together.

Inside there's Kerry and Keith looking tired, but glad to see Mac and Billy arrive.

'Nice to have you back' Kerry says to Billy as she gives him a hug.

'You sure you're not just glad I'm in so you can go home?'

'Hey cheeky I'm not that heartless' she replies. 'It only seems like yesterday when you started, but look at ya now...Got your feet settled under the table alright.'

Billy just smiles, thinking: how little the others know about what's really going on in his mind. Only Mac knows how seriously he's thinking of leaving.

'Kerry, with two feisty lassies on station he's gotta learn quickly to stand up for himself' Mac tells her.

'I've no idea what you mean Mac' Kerry replies innocently.

'Nae Kerry, of course not. Give us ye radios and get ya self home to bed; where you can catch up on your dreams of being innocent.' Taking their radios, Mac and Billy put their kit on 0642, ready to go. 'Time for another McDamnock brew I think Billy' Mac says as they walk back into the mess room.

'Oh dear' Billy thinks to himself. *'Forgot about Mac's tea, I've not missed that.'* Just then their radios go off, for what would have been a very late job for the night crew if they weren't in to take over. *'Well at least I'll get out of the tea then'* he thinks as they turn around and make their way back out to 0642.

'You want me to attend Billy, let you get back into the swing of things slowly' Mac asks.

'That'll be good...Thanks Mac' a relieved Billy replies, worried that Mac would have wanted him to jump right back in.

'So what we got then this early in the morning' Mac says while pressing mobile on the Terrific. Looking at the screen he reads the details out 'It's a thirty two year old female in labour and waters have broken. Nice and easy job for us Billy, don't want any dramas now do we.'

'Think I've had my fill of that for a while Mac' Billy says as he puts 0642's gear lever into drive. Then putting his foot down they make their way down the lane, out of the station and through Casildon-On-the-Hill's high street. The sun burns through the haze and rises up into the sky as 0642 makes its way to its destination. As Billy drives he thinks about the last couple of months working with Mac, learning: *'The ways of the road'* as Mac used to call it. Or figuring out what a *'tartan trumpet'* was.

'You ok Billy?' Mac asks.

'Yep all ok at the mo Mac' comes his reply.

'Looks like it's gonna be a bonnie day today, I feel it in my boots Billy, not a cloud in the sky...Any problems or worries you just let old Mac know ok.'

'Will do' Billy replies.

Approaching the address Billy turns the blues off. The house is a large detached property and big enough for Billy to park 0642 on the gravel drive. They take the usual grab bag and Entonox, plus a maternity pack in with them. 'Just in case' Mac says. At the door they're greeted by a man looking very anxious. 'Oh am I glad to see you gentlemen' his trembling voice says. 'Please...Come this way she's upstairs.'

Walking up the stairs they begin to hear the familiar sounds of a woman with labour pains. At the top of the large landing there's no need to ask for directions in which way to go, they follow the familiar screams of a woman in labour to the room where their patient is. Lying on the bed she's propping herself up on her elbows. Half dressed, she's got a towel covering her modesty.

'Morning lass, what's your name' Mac asks.

'Hannah' she says in-between panting.

'How many weeks pregnant are you?'

'Thirty eight plus six' she manages to say.

'Ok lassie start taking some Entonox. Is this first or second bairn?'

Hannah holds up three fingers while breathing in the gas and biting down on the mouthpiece.

'What time did her contractions start' Mac asks her husband who's standing by the door looking nervous.

'Erm...it was erm...' he tries to answer, but can't think straight. His hands flapping at his sides as he tries to remember.

'Thirty minutes ago' Hannah shouts out, dropping the mouthpiece out of her mouth and quickly picking it up and putting it back in.

'Yes that's it' he answers. 'I was gonna take her in the car, dropping the two girls off at my mum's on the way. I've rung maternity they were expecting us, but when Hannah got up her waters broke. Just there she stood right next to my golf club bag, next to where your colleague's standing now.'

Billy looks at the floor and takes a step sideways. He thinks back to Mac's advise on his first maternity *'A lassie's first bairn will take longer, but once they've dropped that first one, anymore will come on out with just a wee cough,'* Billy realises that they probably aren't going anywhere right now.

'Aaaah' Hannah screams again, as another contraction begins. 'I'm feeling the need to push' she screams out.

'Ok Hannah' Mac says. 'I need to have a look to see if baby's crowning yet, is that ok?'

'Yes just get on with it and get this bloody baby out' she shouts back at him; now that she's reminded how painful this stage of labour feels like for the third time.

'We're not there just yet, a wee while longer' Mac tells her after checking. He's just about to ask Billy to ring maternity and request a midwife attends when he has a thought. 'Billy will you take over for a moment please while I phone maternity.' A little reluctant Billy kneels down by Hannah and coaches her through the contractions. 'Morning Casildon maternity' Mac says as stands out in the hallway calling the labour ward. 'Paramedic McDamnock TC here with a patient booked in with yourselves who was on her way up to yous this morning.'

'Ah yes I took the call are they still on their way?'

'Unfortunately no, there's been a change of plan and the little bairn's on its way out now. Can we have a midwife attend the home address please.'

'Ok' she replies. 'I think there's actually one of our community midwifes just booked on duty in that area. I'll ask her to go straight round to you.'

'Aye that's grand lassie.'

At that moment Hannah's husband passes Mac again in the hall as he's aimlessly going to and fro without getting anything done. 'Young man can you turn the heating on and place a baby grow on the radiator please,' he asks the flustered husband.

'Ok erm...erm...where are they luv' he asks Hannah as he makes his way back into the bedroom.

'Where they've been for the last bloody week Gary, the dining room by the cabinet' she shouts at him. 'And check on the girls Gary...Gary did you hear me...Aaaah' as another contraction starts.

'How we doing lad, you ok?' Mac shouts out to Billy from the hallway.

'I'm ok, but I think Hannah's contractions are getting stronger.'

'Why you say that then?' he asks walking back into the bedroom.

'Because Hannah's squeezing my hand even tighter nooow' as another contraction begins.

Hannah's grip on Billy's hand increases as her contractions get stronger and closer together. And as Mac is senior clinician; he keeps an eye on Billy as he guides Hannah through the next stage of the delivery which judging by Hannah's very audible contraction pains; won't be much longer.

Gary comes back up with the baby-grow.

'I've got it' he says excitedly to Hannah. 'Erm...what did you want me to do with it again?'

'Shove the bloody thing up your aaaah'... Hannah screams at him as another contraction begins.

'Fella put it on the radiator for us please' Mac tells him.

Now in a lot of pain and having no patience for Gary, Hannah starts giving her husband some advice.

'You are never coming near me again! Gary you hear me. Ouch...Ouch...I've gotta push' Hannah says loud in an angry voice.

'Lass ease off the gas now so you've got more energy to push' Mac tells her. Then looking at Gary who doesn't know whether to stay in the bedroom or aimlessly pace up and down the hallway again, Mac asks: 'Come round this side fella and hold Hannah's hand before she squeezes my crewmate's off...Hannah's gonna need lots of help and encouragement now.'

'Ok but I've no idea what to say or do...I missed the birth of our first two.'

'Well you're not gonna miss this one!' Hannah tells him through gritted teeth.

It's not long before Gary's squeezed hand matches Billy's, looking extremely pale as Hannah squeezes it while bearing down during the pain of another contraction.

'That's it Hannah' Billy tells her. 'Now push...'Go on you can do it. That's it keep going... keep going. Ok now pant Hannah, you need to pant' he tells her as the contraction starts to subside.

'That's easy for you to say!' she stressfully replies. 'Oh it's ok for you, you're not going through what I am, God I forgot how painful this felt. Gary I never wanna hear about your man flu again, you hear me!...Aaaah' she screams, as she starts bearing down again.

'That's it good, keep going' Billy tells her trying to reassure Hannah that it's all ok. 'Keep going, you're doing really well.'

With the next two pushes, the baby's head, is now crowning. 'OUCH, that f...... hurts now.'

'Hannah we're nearly there now, the baby's head is out...Now pant, you must pant Hannah!'

Hannah looks at Gary and gives a little cry and a tear runs down her emotional face. But that look quickly turns to one of anger as she crushes his hand even tighter; screaming out in pain. Billy's feeling really nervous now as he says to her: 'I need to check the cord's not in the way, keep panting for me don't push yet.'

Mac kneels down next to Billy and leans over him. Keeping an eye on his performance he whispers 'You're doing well lad, doing well.' Then looks up at their patient 'that's it Hannah, you're doing well too.'

'Ok Hannah, with the next push' Billy says hoping this is the one. 'I want you to keep it going as long as you can.'

As the urge begins to come over Hannah to push; all three men start encouraging her to keep going. 'That's it go on Hannah you can do it, keep on going, keep going,' they all say. 'That's it, keep going.'

Suddenly...At 06:42 with a gush of amniotic fluid sprayed over Billy's shirt; a newborn baby arrives into this world. Billy's hands gently encase the newborn as it's delivered and he brings it up to mum's abdomen.

'Hannah look' Gary says excitedly, 'It's a boy.'

'You didn't know what sex the bairn was?' Mac asks.

'No, Hannah didn't want to find out till the birth as we've got two girls. She wanted to hold onto the hope it was gonna be a boy.'

'Congratulations to you both' Billy says as he wipes their new addition dry. Then after cutting the cord; this time with ease, he wraps him up in a baby towel before passing him to mum.

Hannah holding baby wrapped in his first baby towel in her arms, now feels worn out. But manages to say: 'I'm sorry if I was shouting at the two of you.'

'Oh that's ok' Billy replies.

'What about me then?' Gary asks as he strokes their new-born's head.

'Well as you've given me a boy, I'm sorry for shouting at you too.' Hannah's face smiles as she looks content with the glow of a new mum. Gary kisses his wife on the forehead and they both gaze at their son. Then Hannah looks up at Billy and stares at him for a moment, her breathing now slowed down she asks: 'What's your name?'

'Billy' he replies worried he's done something wrong.

'That's perfect' she whispers to herself and then looks at Gary 'I want to call him Billy.'

Gary Nods with agreement 'that sounds perfect.'

Looking back at Billy Hannah asks: 'What do you think Billy; is that alright with you?'

He wipes a tear from his eye and swallows before he can speak. 'Thank you, that's very kind of you.'

Mac stands back, leaning against the wall by the bedroom door with his arms folded; he has a big grin on his face as he watches them. Too wrapped up in Hannah's newborn; only Mac hears a knock at the door. 'That'll be the midwife, I'll go and let her in' he says walking out of the bedroom, but they don't hear him.

Downstairs he's greeted by the midwife. 'Well hello again.'

'Marion, so nice to see you on this bonnie morning' Mac replies. He gives her a handover before going upstairs; allowing the three of them to enjoy the moment with Hannah and Gary's newborn. Then at the bedroom door, he knocks before entering. 'Don't wanna spoil the moment, but the midwife's here now.' After introducing Marion to Hannah Mac starts to tidy up their mess. 'Billy you rest for a bit, I sort this lot out.' Collecting all their equipment together; he takes it back down to 0642 while Marion checks mum and baby over.

A few minutes later Billy joins him in the ambulance. Mac's Sat down filling in his paperwork, Billy sits next to him with a smile on his face that Mac hasn't seen for a long time. 'You did a good job there Billy, I'm proud of you.'

'I didn't expect that' he replies still surprised.

'Aye this job definitely has some strange moment's laddie, come on lets go see if we're still needed' he says as tears off the paperwork.

Upstairs Marion's holding the newborn Billy. 'I think you boys can go back for a clean-up and cup of tea' she tells them. 'I'll look after Hannah and the baby.'

As they say goodbye, Hannah asks: 'Billy can I have a photo of you holding my Billy.'

Sat there holding little Billy in his arms he feels so proud to have delivered this little man into the world who will now carry his name. And as Hannah asks Mac to join in for another photo, he thinks about his own dislike of his name in the past: *'Maybe Billy's not such a bad name after all.'*

'Give us the keys Billy' Mac says to him as they walk across the gravel driveway towards 0642. 'Put ya feet up, old Mac will drive us back'

'Thanks Mac' he says passing him the keys and opening the passenger door.

As they drive off Billy answers the radio: '0642 we're clear but yellow. Need to return to restock and change uniform.'

'Roger 0642 return, I'll book you out of service. Let us know when you're available.'

Driving back down the country lanes Billy looks out of the window and stares at the blue sky. He's filled with emotion and thoughts of the past three months, the good memories and the bad ones flow through his mind. He looks out at the folk of Casildon-On-The-Hill who are up and about; starting off on their normal humdrum daily business. He thinks about how much he's already done on this sunny morning before their day's even begun. And, how enriched his life has been made by the events of this morning's incident that they've attended.

Back at Casildon Ambulance station there's only Dickie there, he's pottering around as normal as 0642 pulls up in the yard. The two get out and walk into the garage. Dickie as usual is in a world of his own and not looking where he's going as he nearly bumps into Billy.

'Sorry fella didn't see you there' he says as he looks at the state of Billy's shirt. 'Oh dear what happened to you?'

'Me Billy's been a busy boy Dickie...A busy boy' Mac says.

Billy goes into the men's changing room to change his shirt, while Mac gets rid of their clinical waste and restocks the vehicle. As Billy puts on his spare shirt he realises he'd forgotten to show it the iron before bringing it to work. *'Oh well too late now'* he thinks to himself. Walking back out of the changing room he hears Mac calling out 'Want a brew Billy?'

'Please' he replies, then realises *'Oh no it'll be a McDamnock special brew won't it,* but entering the messroom for what he expects to be a mug filled with the usual dark brown fluid, Mac hands him a mug of normal looking tea. Billy looks up confused.

'Missus McDamnock's been nagging me about making tea too strong for you, so here you go one that's bound to be a wee bit more to your liking. And besides, that rubber plant ain't looking too good these days. What...Did you think you're the only one who's wasted a McDamnock brew down that thing?

'Mmm...that's not bad Mac' Billy says taking a slurp from it. 'Not bad at all' as he sits down.

'Aye to you it might, but I like mine a bit more northern looking in colour, compared to you southern folk.'

Sat down at the table they sit in silence. Billy leaning back in his chair; wearing his creased un-ironed shirt, he still has a big smile across his face.

'We'll let the twallys know we're green and available in a minute' Mac breaks the silence with. Then leaning forward he softly says 'Billy always remember; after disaster there's some kind of hope. After death, there's birth...Though we may not see both of these close together very often, remember those hopes and births and hang onto them. Keep those thoughts with you Billy, they'll help you understand and see you through the darker times.' He leans back in his chair and gives Billy a wink. Just then the radio goes off. 'Guess they wanna know if we're available yet' Mac says as he picks the radio up off his belt clip. 'Naught sex for two' he answers in the usual McDamnock manner.

'I know you're busy 0642, just wondering how you're getting on?' despatch ask.

'Standby one' Mac tells them and puts the radio down on the table. He leans forward again towards Billy: 'Well Billy what do you think...Do you think you're ready?'

The end...Of part 1.

Dedicated to all Ambulance staff up and down the country and all over the world. Whether in a control room or on the front line; all face a constant battle under pressure twenty four hours a day, seven days a week of high demand, with only limited resources to help people in need of medical assistance.

Please respect the 999 emergency services.

Thank you for reading and thanks to all the staff that have contributed towards making this story. Part 2 **True life & death tales** is available on Amazon

If you enjoyed this true tale, please pass it on to others.

The hope is for one day to gain production interest for a mini television drama.

Twitter: #McDamnock

Facebook: https://www.facebook.com/True-Blue-Light-Tales

Many thanks,

McDamnock TC.

Printed in Great Britain
by Amazon